Champion
of the
Heart

JULIE PARKER

This is a work of fiction. Names, characters, places, and incidents are products of the author's imagination or are used fictitiously and are not to be construed as real. Any resemblance to actual events, locations, organizations, or persons, living or dead, is entirely coincidental.

World Castle Publishing, LLC
Pensacola, Florida
Copyright © Julie Parker 2020
Paperback ISBN: 9781951642976
eBook ISBN: 9781951642983
First Edition World Castle Publishing, LLC, August 3, 2020
http://www.worldcastlepublishing.com
Licensing Notes
Cover: Karen Fuller
Editor: Maxine Bringenberg

DEDICATION

For my mom, Marilyn.
Thank you for all your encouragement
through every stage of this story.
This one's for you.

PROLOGUE

ENGLAND, 1334

Sounds of rowdy laughter and drunken boasts assailed the old servant's ears as she crept silently past the entrance of the great hall. She hastened towards the heavy doors with her burden clutched tightly in her grip, not wishing to draw undesired attention toward herself. It was unlikely the group of miscreants would take note of her, though, so great were they engaged in their own depths of debauchery.

With effort driven by desperation, she was able to force the heavy doors open wide enough to give her leave to venture through. She forced her gait to be steady, denying her legs the urge to take flight in the unlikely event she may be seen leaving the castle at such an hour. She was not overly surprised to pass through the yard unchallenged, but for once felt gratitude that the indolent guards were again not at their post. The portcullis was raised high in defiance that none were considered a threat to the great and powerful Lord Edwin Madmont, and she passed beneath it, releasing a breath of relief.

The land was dark, and the trees cast sinister shadows in her path as she turned off the roadway she followed and stepped into the forest. She walked on, careful of the bundle she carried, as her legs brought her closer to her destination. The moon finally broke free of the clouds and gifted the night with an eerie brightness. The trees began to thin as the old woman came upon a clearing and began to climb the slope of the hill before her. Mist swirled at her feet and danced around the large stone columns that glinted like steel swords angled up towards the sky. A wolf bayed in the distance, and her steps faltered now with a tinge of fear. She moved to the center of the circle the ancient stones formed and knelt upon the earth. Laying down the bundle she carried, she stretched out her hands wide above her head.

Her lips moved in prayer, and as the words were spoken, her tears flowed freely. She was suddenly angered with the unjustness of the world around her. A world in which the innocent were punished and evil ran wild with unleashed abandon. She cried out with despair over the treacherous fate the poor child before her had been served.

She gave the child one last look of regret and then rose up slowly. She feared to linger lest she be missed, and dared not call any attention to the deed she had done this night. As the child within the blanket began to emit a sad, soft cry, the old woman lifted her and placed her behind one of the stones to hide her from sight. As she crept back toward the forest, she did not see the shadowed figure that approached the stones behind her.

CHAPTER 1

ENGLAND, 1350

The ground shook with tremors as the leaves joined in a fierce dance with the wind. Gemma stood stock-still and raised her arms slowly into the air, fingers stretched wide. Her slim hips swung to a rhythm only her gifted ears could detect. She chanted—ancient words from a people as old as the land itself. People time had forgotten, or so she hoped. She was taking a chance, relying upon the thunder and fierce wind to shield her plea to the gods from curious, prying eyes. Desperation had forced her hand this treacherous eve—she knew she must succeed.

Lowering her hands, she bowed her head in silent prayer. Gemma dropped to her knees, then placed her hands upon the damp soil beneath her. She bent her head and pressed her lips to the ground. Rising, she backed away from the shadow of the ancient stones and made her way through the forest. This night's work was over, at least for now. She would return when and if the opportunity presented itself again.

Chilled by the dampness of her dress, she hurried through the forest and returned to her cottage. She entered the tiny bedroom and removed her gown, then crawled beneath the thin blanket on her bed to lie upon the straw mattress. As soon as she lay her head down, she was fast asleep.

As she slept, she dreamed. Dreamed of one day finding safety, finding love. It was a dream she had had of late. One full of rainbows and beautiful rushing waterfalls, flowers, and endless green fields. Fields of hope. And the strong, handsome warrior, riding on his magnificent black steed. He would ride toward her, coming closer and closer, but alas, never near enough for her to fully see his face. Tonight, his face once again eluded her. It, like this dream of hers, was shrouded in mystery.

The light of the morning sun crept through the shutters of the window into the bedroom of the small cottage. Gemma awakened and sat up quickly. She rose and opened the chest at the end of the bed and pulled out a gown to wear. It was well worn and mended, as were her other two gowns, but it was clean. Donning the dress, she drew a comb through her long mass of dark hair that reached just below her hips, before fashioning a hasty braid. She then headed through the door to the front room. A hard loaf of bread on the table was the only food left to eat. Taking it, she picked up her cloak and satchel, unbarred the door, and went outside.

The air was warm, and only a few clouds were in the sky. Branches were strewn across the faint pathway, and small puddles were the only telltale signs of the havoc wreaked by the storm the night before. After making her way to a small rushing creek, she sat by the water's edge to finish her bread. Cupping her hands, she drank. She sat for a time, contemplating the trek she must make to the nearby village. Beset by anxiety, she was not just a little frightened of what awaited her.

Her journey there was one of desperation. Her meager stock of supplies had recently been depleted after a long, hard winter, a cold spring, and a summer that had seen such storms that her small garden was repeatedly washed away. Nothing remained except a few vegetables and a small amount of grain. Finding aid was imperative, or she would not survive. As she rose and began to walk, ideas formed in her head, thoughts of anything she could do to make herself useful to the villagers.

Her healing skills, though feared, were still grudgingly appreciated by some. Even the most skeptical came looking for her when it came time to deliver a child into the world, or if someone was ailing or hurt.

Gemma reached the edge of the forest and began the trek down the narrow dirt road that led into the village. Luck was on her side this day — the road was deserted. No doubt the peasants were busy cleaning up after the night's storm.

The village consisted of about sixty or so peasants. There was a mill, smithy, church, and several small huts and cottages. In the past, the peasants had been quite prosperous due to successful crops and had no difficulty paying rents to their lord. This year would be different. Heavy rains had ruined several crops, and last year's stores were depleted. Finding help for herself among them would prove difficult.

As Gemma made her way through the village, she caught sight of a large group of men attempting to remove a giant old tree that had fallen upon the roof of the church. They had fastened one end of a thick rope to the heaviest branch and the other end to a plow ox. They were urging the animal forward by striking it with sticks to pull the heavy weight of the tree. The ox valiantly pulled, but then balked at the strenuous effort. The tree was lodged too tightly, and unwilling to surrender its resting place so easily.

Gemma watched, fearful for the animal at the brutal insistence of the peasants to keep pulling. Rushing forward, unmindful of the startled and angry glares and shouts from the men, she placed her hands lightly aside the ox's head and looked deeply into its eyes. She leaned forward and whispered encouragement into its ear. Moments later, the ox responded to her. It again pulled at the rope with all its strength. The tree began to move. The harder the animal pulled, the farther the tree came forward, until it finally released its grip on the roof and fell to the waiting ground below.

The men cheered. They clasped each other's hands and slapped each other on the back. Then they turned their attention to Gemma. Their shouts of joy ceased, their smiles faded, replaced by scorn and anger.

"What witch's trick did you use upon the animal, Gemma?"

It was more of an accusation than a question aimed at her by the largest man in the group. She recoiled at the verbal assault.

"Just kindness and calm words is what you witnessed here, Daniel. Naught else." Since her gran's death, the animals of the forest had become like family to her and helped ease the loneliness in her isolated world. But now she once again had put herself on the receiving end of anger and suspicion. This was not what she had planned when coming to the village. She came to seek aid, not breed distrust. She attempted to look demure, lowering her eyes to the ground. "I am sorry for interfering with the ox. I meant no harm."

Another man stepped menacingly toward her and looked down upon her with disgust. "What do you want? We have not called for your services this day."

Her gaze took in the men gathered around her, and she felt a shudder of fear. "Please, good sirs. I have come forth seeking employment. I am a healer, as you know, but I can also earn my keep doing other things."

"What kind of 'other things' do you have in mind?"

one of the men jeered.

"Well," she replied, ignoring the rude suggestion. "I could work in your homes and help your good wives with mending or washing. Or I could help in the fields, as harvest time is upon you."

The men laughed at her suggestions. They turned away from her and began the work of removing the tree, making good use of the axes they had brought along. Only Daniel remained. He looked hard at her, then he too turned his back and began to work.

Gemma stepped toward him as he grasped his axe and placed her hands firmly upon his arm. "Please, Daniel, do not turn away from me. I can be useful if someone would just give me a chance."

He gazed upon her small hands, clinging to him desperately. He pulled out of her grasp as if burned by her touch. Quietly he spoke to her. "Go to my home. I have work to do now, but I will return this evening. See if you can make yourself useful until that time."

"My thanks, Daniel. I promise I will prove to be a help to you. You will not regret this."

Gemma sped off in the direction of his home. When she reached the small cottage at the end of the roadway, she walked up the overgrown path. Not taking the time to notice the rough state of the place, she pushed open the wooden door and stepped inside. Squinting into the dimly lit room, her gaze slowly took in her surroundings. She stepped further inside, wondering how anyone could live like this. The room was disgraceful.

It was obvious the dwelling lacked a feminine touch. Daniel was still a devout bachelor. The cottage consisted of two rooms, much like her own in the forest, but that was where the similarities ended. The bigger of the two rooms had a heavy wooden table placed before the hearth. The table was littered with filthy bowls containing bits of uneaten food. There were wooden cups scattered about, with trace amounts of water or ale inside. The floor was dirt, as was her own, but his was covered with filthy rags and garbage. Despite the sorry state of the place, she smiled. There was plenty of work to keep her busy here for days.

Most of the day was spent putting the cottage back in order. By late afternoon, Gemma turned her thoughts to what she could make Daniel for supper. She had always helped Gran prepare the meals they shared. Spending time together as they worked side by side was one of the fond memories she would cherish forever. Searching out the croft for vegetables to place in the cauldron that hung over the hearth, she found some cabbage, leeks, an onion, and a bit of garlic. There was even a little rabbit meat under a cloth in a bowl on the table. She added everything to the pot, along with some water, and before long, she had a fine smelling stew brewing.

The sun was just beginning to set when Daniel returned home. A look of surprise lit his face when he surveyed the order of the cottage.

She smiled as she dished out some of the stew into a waiting bowl. "Greetings, Daniel."

"Greetings," he replied, taking a seat at the table.

She placed a bowl of the fragrant stew and a hunk of stale bread in front of him. He gratefully began to partake of his meal and motioned for her to serve some up for herself and join him at the table. They enjoyed their food together in silence, and after Daniel finished his third helping, he pushed his bowl away and leaned back in his chair.

"That was one of the finest meals I have had in a long time."

Gemma was happy with Daniel's praise and hopeful he would wish her to return. He got up from the chair and strode about the room, noticing the changes she had wrought. He seemed satisfied with her work, so she hesitantly approached him.

"I would like to continue to work for you tomorrow. There is still much to be done." Daniel gazed upon her thoughtfully while she added quickly, "All I would ask of you in return is some food and perchance some coin if you could spare it."

He seemed to consider her offer for a moment, then nodded. "I will agree to your bargain."

"Then, I shall see you tomorrow." She smiled her relief as she gathered up her satchel and cloak.

She headed toward the door and turned as Daniel said, "To tomorrow then, Gemma."

As she went to leave, she thought she detected a glint of heat smoldering in his eyes. But as she made her way down the path to the roadway, she decided it was likely just a flicker of light from one of the candles that had caught his eye.

She walked through the village on the roadway that wound towards the forest and her cottage. The village was blessedly quiet, the peasants having their supper and retiring early after the long day. Entering the forest, she headed to the stream she had visited earlier in the day and sat down again at the edge to drink the cool water.

She thought of her efforts and success. Not only would helping Daniel with his home bring her much needed supplies but hopefully, being amongst the villagers daily might just bring them to finally accept her.

Returning to her cottage, she performed her evening ablutions and retired to her cot. Falling fast asleep, she was again claimed by her enchanting dreams.

She found herself at the mysterious standing stones dancing in the moonlight. Her hair flew about her as she twirled around the colossal formations in a wild dance. Suddenly the earth shook with such a force that she was thrown to the ground. From beyond the mist, he came. The warrior emerged through the fog on his giant steed. He thundered towards her faster and faster, steam blowing from the massive destrier's nostrils as the warrior urged him onward.

Gemma lay motionless but soon rose up on her knees.

The animal was gaining ground and would soon be upon her. She must flee. But her body would not respond to her mind's command to take flight. Frozen, she could only stare in horrified fascination as the warrior fast approached. Eyes shut tight, she awaited the pounding of the massive hooves. Any moment now, she feared she was fated to meet her demise.

But the moment did not come.

Slowly she opened her eyes, and there before her, barely a hand-span away, was the horse, its long legs rooted to the spot. She raised her eyes up the length of the beast and took in the huge warrior atop him. A giant of a man, he was in full combat gear, as though he sought to do battle this eve. The moonlight glinted off the metal of his visor—it seemed his face would forever remain hidden from her. Still, he was here before her. Never had she been so close to him. She would not waste this precious chance. She would speak to this man and finally uncover the mystery of who he was and why he haunted her dreams.

Gemma cautiously rose to her feet so as not to startle the beast before her. As she opened her lips to form the words she had longed to speak, the warrior drew back on the reins. The destrier reared up, barely missing her, whirled around, and thundered back through the fog. Strength finally found her legs, and she tore after him. She shouted and begged him to return, but her effort was for naught. He had vanished, disappearing into the night as quickly as he had come.

She awoke to the dawn casting a light glow through her open window. She dressed quickly, for today she had a task to attend to. Last night's dream only vaguely entered her thoughts as she hurriedly donned her cloak and left the cottage. Today she did not linger at the stream's edge but quickly drank her fill then went on her way. The village soon came into view, and she was a little dismayed to see the peasants streaming about. The men, women, and children went hard about their work, barely turning a glance towards her as she made her way by.

This did not overly surprise her — there was much work in the fields to be done. The peasants were intent on harvesting what was salvageable while the weather remained dry. The past week's rain had destroyed most of the wheat in the largest field. The other fields had not fared much better. As she passed the workers, she hoped they were able to recover enough from the soaking fields to appease their lord. If they did not, she hoped their lord would take pity on them and not demand too much of a levy.

As if her thoughts had conjured them, she heard approaching riders. Gemma slowed her pace as she walked past the fields and the peasants at work. As she watched, the riders came closer, and finally, she could distinguish their garb. They wore the colors of black and gold with the crest of the leopard, clearly identifying them as the lord's men. She was not the only one to take note of the sudden arrival of the soldiers. The peasants had ceased their work and were openly staring at the unwanted visitors.

Gemma knew it was the lord's bailiff come to collect the rents owing. She hid behind a tree and watched from the edge of the field as the men approached the villagers. Sitting atop his palfrey, the bailiff removed a rolled parchment from his cloak.

"Hear me, people of Haddon. I have been sent forth by Lord de Bohon to collect the rents." As he spoke, he unrolled the parchment and began to read off the list of required goods.

As he read, the villagers began to gasp, and then gave voice to their grievance all at once. The bailiff, angry at the interruption, glared at the crowd, clearly displeased. An old man, Alfred, the village reeve, stepped forward. The crowd quieted when he raised his hand for silence. He hesitantly approached the bailiff.

"Please, my lord, the amounts ye read off would have been readily given in previous years. But of late, the weather has delivered much havoc in the fields, and the crops have been sorely ravaged. Please allow us more time so we may make our lord a better presentation."

The bailiff regarded the old man coldly. "Do you think you can live upon these lands for nothing? The summer now comes to an end—it is time for collection of what is owed to the lord. I come to collect his due, not to return with your sorry excuses."

"Just a little more time, my lord, is all we ask. I beseech ye."

The bailiff stood firm, his hard stare brooking no leniency. The peasants in the field were becoming angry at his high-handedness. They began to form together, their voices outraged and loud. Scythes were grasped in hands, becoming crude weapons. They looked ready for battle, much to the dismay of Alfred. The three soldiers who had accompanied the bailiff spread out before the riotous group at his swift gesture. They put their hands upon the hilts of their swords in readiness for a fight.

Gemma took in the scene before her in fear. What would become of these poor peasants? The soaking fields would barely yield enough subsistence to last the villagers throughout the winter. Giving over his share to the lord would deplete their meager supplies by nearly half. Surely the Lord of Haddon could be reasonable. He must realize that taking so much from the villagers would leave them destitute, and then who would he have to work his fields next year? A bunch of half-starved peasants would be good for naught.

The villagers began shouting and arguing with the bailiff, swinging their scythes around. The man must not have been expecting such outright refusal and anger from them, or he would have surely brought with him a stronger force of men. As it stood, nothing would be accomplished this day. With all the shouting going on, Gemma was amazed the soldiers could follow the bailiff's command to retreat.

The peasants cheered when the bailiff quit the field, followed by the soldiers. The victory would be short-lived, however, for there was no doubt they would return. Alfred's gaze at the men and women around him was sorrowful. Gemma could hear his attempt to get the people to return to their work.

"There is much labor to be done yet, good fellows. Aye, ye have won the day, but the morrow will bring a greater challenge. We must present our lord with an honest showing of our hard work, and mayhap he will be satisfied with our offer, small though it may be." The villagers voiced their agreement with the old man's wise words and put their scythes to the fields, returning to their work.

Gemma was thoughtful as she walked to Daniel's cottage. She had not seen Daniel amongst the other workers in the fields. She wondered if he still might be abed as she strolled up the weedy trail to his cottage. As she rapped lightly on the door, she looked at the overgrown path and thought this may be a good task to tackle on the morrow.

After a few moments, the door finally creaked open. Daniel stood before her, dressed and ready to leave for the day's labors. They exchanged greetings, and he went on his way. She pushed the happenings at the field to the back of her mind. It wouldn't help her now to worry about what would happen on the morrow when the bailiff returned.

Gemma spent her day much as she had the day before. She had set to work on the pile of bedding and clothing, mending and washing, barely completing the heavy task before again having supper waiting for Daniel when he returned home at dusk. She dished out the heated stew into two bowls and sat at the table while she waited for him to wash the day's dust from his hands and face. He soon joined her at the table, taking the stool across from her. After finishing another three helpings of the stew, he drank back his ale and refilled his cup.

"Do you wish more ale?" he asked.

"No. I thank you, but I must see to cleaning these dishes and be on my way."

He grasped her wrist playfully as she went about the task of clearing the table. "There is enough time for cleaning up later, Gemma. But now, there are better things to do this eve."

She snatched her hand away. "What are you about, Daniel? I have no time for play." Again, she attempted to clear away the dishes as Daniel broodingly watched her.

"Come now, woman. I just wish a little conversation after a long day spent in the fields."

Glaring at him in exasperation, Gemma replied, "The hour grows late, and I too am weary from a day long spent caring for your neglected home. I vow I do not know how one man could create such work." Putting the used dishes aside, she went to the door and removed her cloak from the peg. Donning it, she turned to him. "I will finish cleaning up tomorrow, as we are both too weary to be good company this night."

She made her way out and closed the door behind her. She could tell by Daniel's tone that he, too, was worried about what had happened with the bailiff. There was no doubt he had heard about the tense exchange today.

When she approached her cottage, almost full darkness was upon the evening. A faint light shone from the partial moon and many stars in the sky. She'd known the moon had been full the night she had sought guidance at the stones, though she had not actually seen it. The night had been full of darkness and merciless rains. The heavens had shown their might and displeasure. It was a miracle any good had come of that night's work. But it had. Now she had a place in the village. A precarious one, but one, nonetheless. She now had hope for her future.

Gemma retired to bed, and as she lay alone in the dark, last night's dream entered her thoughts. The dream had felt so real, as though the warrior and his massive destrier had stood before her at the great standing stones.

Why had they come so close to her last night, and why at her place of worship? Was the warrior somehow, someway, reaching out to her? Across time and space, breaching her very dreams, trying to warn her?

~*~

In the distance, resting upon the land like a great stone giant, was Haddon Castle. Lord Tristan de Bohon, the overlord of the surrounding land and village, stood atop the battlements and observed the night. As the sentry passed by, he gave his lord a nod of his head in acknowledgment. Tristan's nightly haunts were well known throughout the castle by its inhabitants.

"It is quiet this eve, my lord," the sentry said to Tristan as he made another pass atop the wall.

"Aye, that it is, John. It would appear all's well," Tristan replied. "Although, I have heard there is more trouble amongst the peasants. I am beginning to tire of their constant complaining." He sighed wearily as he ran an agitated hand through his hair.

"That does seem to be the way of it of late, my lord. The peasants crying foul with the weather so as not to pay their rents."

When Cedric, Tristan's bailiff, had returned, he'd relayed to his lord how the peasants had balked. In lieu of giving over a share of their crops, they had offered up excuses and hollow promises of future presentment instead. They had also taken a stand against his men and driven them off with threat of violence. This had put Tristan in a precarious position. In the spring, he had heard much complaining, but never had he met with such open defiance when dealing with the villagers. Although, he admitted to himself, the weather had been quite merciless of late.

He bid the sentry good eve and descended the stairway of the battlements to the third floor. He followed the passageway to the main staircase, which took him down to the first floor of the castle. Once below, he could hear the shouts of rowdy merriment, and he followed the sound into the great hall.

It did not surprise him overmuch to see a group of men seated about one of the tables. He noted grimly that his two brothers were amongst them. The laughter was loud and rang out, grating on his nerves. *By God, have they nothing better to do than end each night in drink?* He stalked forward and took up a hardened stance behind his two errant brothers. Giles, the older of the two, and Denton, the youngest male of the family, sat blissfully unaware of their eldest brother's displeasure.

One of the men distinctly cleared his throat, and catching the questioning glances from the two brothers, nodded his head in the direction behind them. Giles and Denton cautiously turned around on the bench and took in the heated glare of the eldest de Bohon.

"Well, if it is not our lord, come to grace us with his presence," Giles said with a slight slur to his voice.

"Tristan. Come and join us, brother, we would be glad for your company," Denton said, motioning to the empty seat beside him on the bench.

"I think not. It would be wise for someone to retain a clear head this eve. There may be trouble brewing, for the peasants have been uneasy of late, and I would have my wits about me."

His brothers looked up at him sharply, ever the eager

soldiers, at the mention of trouble.

"Think you, Tristan, there may be difficulties ahead?" asked Denton, unable to contain the excitement in his voice.

Tristan took in the hopeful looks of the group of soldiers before him. All of them were hardened warriors. He had fought with these men in past battles, and they were bound by the blood they had shed. They had joined with him to lay claim to Haddon Castle when the king had ordered it be taken. Edward III had deeded it to Tristan, a gift for his loyalty after a victorious battle. But it had come with ulterior intentions as well. Madmont, a traitor to the king, had occupied the castle, and Tristan had to lay siege to attain that which was already rightfully his by royal decree. For days he and his men had strategized the taking of the large and fortified castle. With planning and the help of his handpicked warriors, the mission had met with success. Madmont, though escaped, had been banished, and before the summer's end, Haddon Castle was Tristan's, unquestioned and undisputed by any in England.

Tristan had ruled Haddon Castle for the past year, and he and his men had taken up residence there the day they had overthrown the previous lord. He had shown himself to be a fair and just lord. Most of the castle inhabitants and the peasants thought well of him and had quickly pledged him their allegiance. The only disruption of the monotonous calm days had been the past year's misfortune with the weather. His men had grown increasingly bored with the lack of strife the year had held. A bit of trouble with the nearby village peasants may be just the thing to distract them from the dull days and their lackadaisical habits.

Tristan decided he would set his men to the task of keeping watch over the village. On the morrow, he would send soldiers out on shifts throughout the days and nights to see that the peasants were taken in hand. He felt a show of force would be just the thing to quiet the unrest of the village. His men could quell this sudden uprising and restore order to his lands.

The men around the table had grown thoughtful and looked to him for direction. They would hear him out and act as the soldiers they were. Tristan did then take a seat beside his brother Denton but refused the offer of ale.

"I would have you go to the village," he began. "I would have order restored come the morrow." The men around the table listened with interest to him relaying the problem the bailiff had encountered at the village. Tristan expressed that he did not wish them to strong-arm the peasants into compliance, but to assess the situation and discover a fair alternative. He would still require a contribution to his own dwindling supplies.

After speaking to his men about tomorrow's plans, he rose to leave their company. "I will bid you good eve. I expect to see you all up early, so I suggest you take to your beds as well." He then left the great hall, followed by good eves from the others.

CHAPTER 2

The sun was rising and beginning to warm the morning dew from the lands as Gemma got an early start for the village the next morning. She'd brought along her satchel to replenish her diminishing supply of healing plants, and as she walked, she would stop to inspect choice specimens. Many of the places she had frequented in the past now offered up paltry samples of the usual healthy plants she had found. She knelt by the edge of the forest to inspect a yarrow plant. Though the flowers were slightly wilting, and the leaves were not very large, she still found the sampling to her satisfaction, and carefully plucked it from the earth to put in her satchel. As she rose and began brushing the dirt from her skirts, she paused. Horses were approaching.

She stepped back quickly into the forest and tucked herself down to remain out of sight. As riders passed by where she remained hidden, she could hear their voices. It was not an overly large group, but they were soldiers. She caught a flash of the swords at their sides and made out the black and gold colors identifying them as de Bohon's men. They were heading for the village.

Her caution of the soldiers came from an early age. Gran had always tried to avoid the old lord's soldiers in the past. If on one of their trips to the village, or even walking in the forest, they heard horses or men's voices, they would hide. She continued to hide from the lord's men, from instilled fear.

Their old lord, Edwin Madmont, had been nicknamed "the mad lord" by the villagers. He was a dangerous, evil man, given to heavy drink and oppressive behavior. Gemma had heard whispers of "traitor" about him in the village. It was said that Madmont had betrayed King Edward, and the king had sent forth his favored knight, Lord Tristan, to dispossess him. She knew of the new lord, Tristan de Bohon. Wariness had forced her to remain apprehensive of him. He and his men had captured Haddon Castle last summer, and he had been gifted dominion over the holding. She had heard he was a good man, a fair lord. Yet she had never laid eyes upon him, and she had seen the fierceness of his bailiff and soldiers yesterday when the villagers had rebelled over the rent collection.

The villagers had been fortunate in the past that the weather had been fair. They had been prepared when their old lord, Madmont, would send his men for collection of the rents. Madmont had not been known by any to be a forgiving or kind man, not only in the matter of rent collection but also in the curfew he had instilled upon the village. He and his soldiers used to ride through the village after over-indulging in drink when he had been Lord of Haddon. No one had been safe from Madmont, or from his drunken band of cruel soldiers. They had threatened and terrorized anyone unfortunate enough to be found out on the roads or in the fields after dark.

For these reasons, Gemma remained cautious around soldiers. She had even noticed yesterday in the village that some of the peasants had looked at de Bohon's soldiers uneasily, and some even with expected dread. It would seem that past deeds had bred suspicion and distrust in the minds of the peasants, and that fear had a long memory.

Gemma remained hidden in the woods until the sound of the horses' hooves upon the dirt road and the loud voices of the soldiers faded. Only then did she finally creep from the safety the forest offered. She walked along in the same direction the men had taken, but at a much more remote pace. Her thoughts were no longer on finding the healing plants she needed.

When she entered the village, she noticed the peasants were again hard at work in the fields. The soldiers were not in sight, but she could tell they had indeed passed by from the grim faces of the peasants. As she hiked down the dirt roadway past a group of women laboring in the wheat field, she heard an angry shout.

"Look ye there," a woman said loudly to the group of peasants around her. "Gemma — the witch from the forest. She is the one who brings the devil to our door!"

Gemma froze. She recognized the voice of Judith, a bitter young woman married to a much older man. Judith had approached her and Gran the previous spring and asked them for a potion to aid in keeping her unborn child in her womb full term. She'd been with child then for about a month, but she was worried. Twice before, she had tragically lost the babe after only carrying a few months. Gran had told Judith that she knew of such a potion, but could not promise her it would work for certain. The next day Gemma had returned with it for Judith. Gran did not wish to make the trip a second time. She had begun to tire easily of late, so Gemma had gone alone.

She went to Judith's cottage and gave her a small bag of dried wild raspberry leaves that Gran had told her were an excellent aid in preventing miscarriage. Gemma had shown Judith how to mix a little of the herb in a cup of water to sip in the morning and at bedtime. Judith had thanked her and given her a sack of grain for payment. Sadly, the raspberry leaves did little to help Judith and her unborn child. She lost the babe a week later, and her rage and anger had been aimed at Gemma and Gran. She had accused them of poisoning her and causing her to lose her child. Not many of the villagers had heeded the ranting of the distraught woman, but ever since that time, Gemma and Gran had met with scorn and vindictiveness whenever Judith had been about.

Gemma knew she should keep walking, but her stubborn legs would not cooperate. Judith continued to hurl insults and accusations at her, and some of the other women began to join in. Much to her despair, she noticed the soldiers she had thought gone were now making their way down the roadway toward her and the other women. They must have reached the end of the village, and were heading back toward the castle of Haddon.

Gemma ignored them as they briefly nodded at her and the other women, who had suddenly grown silent, before continuing down the roadway. She then forced herself to turn around to face her accusers. Her fear turned to anger. "Do you think I brought the lord's men here with some witch's power? If I am truly a witch and I am so powerful, then why do I not strike all of you down now?"

Her emotions suddenly overwhelmed her. Always she had helped these people, many times for no payment at all, and in return, they had reviled her and made her feel an outsider. Anger flashed from her green eyes. The hood from her cloak fell back from her dark hair, and the golden torc about her slim neck glinted in the sunlight.

"I have done naught but help many of you and your families when you were ailing or hurt. What do I get in return besides your bitter words and angry stares? Leave me be, and do not bother me again with such vile behavior, or the next time you have need of my skill, I will not be found." She turned on her heel and marched away from the women, all too aware of the gasps and outraged exchanges between them at her angry outburst.

Daniel's cottage came into view, and she was anxious to enter the sanctuary it offered her. She practically ran up the front path and rapped on the door none too lightly. A feeling of defeat washed over her as she recalled the confrontation with the village women. Would she forever be treated as an outcast? She regretted her words now that the moment was over. Her outburst would not gain her the acceptance she craved.

Daniel yanked the door open from within and barely had a chance to offer up a greeting before she pushed her way past him and entered the cottage.

"What is the hurry, Gemma, is there trouble afoot?"

"Nay, Daniel, there is no trouble."

He would learn about the soldiers soon enough, she thought. She turned her back to him and hung up her cloak on the peg to conceal the anxiousness on her face. When she turned back around, she was composed.

"It is a fine day for laboring in the croft. I am anxious to begin is all."

"Oh, aye, that it is. A fine day for laboring in the croft," he agreed distractedly as he pulled on his boots and slung a bag with his mid-day meal over his shoulder. "I am off to the fields. We all must labor hard to fill Lord de Bohon's rent demand. I vow, it shall sorely hurt us to give over so much. There is bare little enough for ourselves." He seemed angry and thoughtful as he strode out the door and stalked down the roadway towards the fields, leaving Gemma staring after him.

After Daniel had departed the cottage, Gemma searched about the kitchen for a large bowl before heading outside. She planned to spend the day working in the croft and was hoping she could attain some semblance of order within the garden. From what she had already seen, it could take her the remainder of the week to set it aright. Weeds were in abundance, almost choking the life from the few vegetable plants. As she set aside the bowl and bent to her task, her mind reflected over what she had witnessed this morn.

Soldiers had come to the village, and the ill effect they had upon the peasants had been immediately apparent. Their very presence had set them on edge. Forced to face some of them upon the roadway, it had looked to her like they were merely giving a silent show of their might. They had done nothing more than ride about the village casually, as though they were assessing the mood of the peasants. She had not noticed the bailiff amongst them, and she wondered if Lord de Bohon had sent forth his men first in caution. The idea that more men may venture from the castle, or that they may do something other than patrol the village peacefully, made her wary.

The morning wore on, and soon the sun was high in the sky. The only reprieve from the heat of the afternoon was the odd cloud covering the land from the sun's scorching rays. Sometimes a cool breeze would brush upon the earth and cause a light blowing of newly fallen leaves.

Gemma sat back on her heels and rubbed a hand across the sweat on her brow. Her throat had become dry after spending most of the day in the croft. She rose up and walked to the well, then pulled up the bucket holding water. Bracing the bucket, she pushed up her sleeves and dove her hands into its depth. She cupped the water and drank deeply before splashing some on her face.

After cooling herself at the well, Gemma entered the cottage, swinging the door shut with her hip. Her arms were filled with the vegetables she had salvaged from the croft. She placed her burden upon the table, then began sorting through her find for what to use for tonight's stew and what to put aside for later use. She retrieved a small dagger from her satchel and began preparing the vegetables for the cauldron.

As she worked, she hummed a tune Gran used to sing to her. The sudden weight of a hand upon her shoulder startled her. She whirled around, dropping her small dagger, shocked and frightened, having thought herself alone. Her fearful stare took a moment to register Daniel's face before recognition washed over her. She stepped back, but the table behind her prevented any further retreat. She looked at his face and saw his eyes inflamed with desire.

"Daniel! What are you about? You frightened me half to death."

She tried to push him away, he stood far too close for comfort. Her small hands shoved at his chest, but she might as well be pushing at an oak tree, for he was very solid.

Daniel easily grasped her wrists with one of his hands. His other hand wrapped around her waist and pulled her forcefully against him. She screamed and tried to break free of his iron grip. She lifted her heel and stomped on his foot, but that only gained her a small grunt from the beast who held her. As he continued his assault upon her, he released her hands, and she flailed about, trying to find anything with which to fight him. Her pitiful blows did nothing to quell him. Then she pulled up her knee—hard—making contact with his manhood. Daniel stilled, then groaned and backed stiffly away, holding himself. His look was fierce, and his teeth bit his bottom lip as he tried to stifle an agonized moan.

Gemma looked across the room to the door, which suddenly seemed leagues away. She swiftly made off for the other side of the table, placing it between her and Daniel's hulking form. Looking down around her ankles, she hoped to find a pot or a fire poker, anything she could use to defend herself. Her eyes came to rest on her small dagger. She made a quick grab for it just as he began to recover himself and started towards her.

She held the dagger before her. "Get back, Daniel! I have no wish to hurt you."

He eyed the little dagger she waved before him and laughed. "Do you think to use that dagger upon me? Come now, Gemma, I have a far larger weapon for you to handle." He lunged over the table.

She sped out of his reach and ran towards the door. As she grappled with the handle, she felt him grab for her arm. He grasped a handful of her dress, and as she pulled away from him, she felt the thin material tear. She screamed and slashed her dagger down his arm. He roared with pain. His hand flew up to cover the wound and came away covered in his blood. As he raged and looked about for a rag, she flung the door wide and raced outside. Her feet tore up the ground as she flew down the roadway through the village.

Daniel was fast upon her. He reached her just as she was passing a field with a few men still at work. The pair began to struggle. He grabbed her arms in a fierce grip and shook her soundly. The villagers took in the scene before them with confusion. They rushed over and forcefully freed Daniel's rough grip from her arms.

"Halt, man! What goes on here?" Niall yelled.

Gemma was shaking with fear, and before she could say a word, Daniel spit out hateful, condemning words.

"She attacked me in my own home!" he lied. "She has worked for me these past few days, and today when I returned early from the fields, I caught her trying to steal from me. When I tried to stop her, she pulled forth her dagger and stabbed me with it!" He shook off the few men who continued to hold him and showed them the bloody slash down his arm.

"Nay!" Gemma yelled. "It did not happen like he says! I was not stealing from him—he came home and attacked me."

She frantically searched the frowning faces of the men for some sign of belief in her. She saw none and knew the battle was lost. These men would never believe her, the witch from the forest, over one of their own.

"I knew there would be trouble inviting this one into our midst, Daniel. Ye should have used more sense, man." Niall spoke to Daniel like he was chastising a child.

"Aye, I know it now. She has played me for a fool, but no longer. I have seen her for the devil's consort she is." He held fast to his injured arm as if to gain pity for the suffering he had received in exchange for his kindness.

Gemma inched back slowly from the men as they spoke. When all eyes momentarily left her, she turned and darted away, her legs pumping furiously at the ground as she sped down the road.

The men gave chase with Daniel in the lead, and he quickly overcame her. He grabbed her arms as she tried to fight him, and she wished in that moment she still held her dagger in her grip. They must have looked like a wild pair, fighting and yelling, both covered in Daniel's blood. That was when the sentries came upon them.

"Halt!" yelled Cedric. "What in the name of God goes on here?"

"Justice, my lord!" Niall was puffing as he came upon the group and answered the man. "That girl attacked the poor man ye see before ye!"

"You there! Unhand that woman," demanded a knight. He dismounted from his horse and moved before them. His eyes first took in Daniel's bloodied arm, and he called back to one of the soldiers to tend the wound. Then his gaze turned to

Gemma. She heard him suck in his breath as he stared at her. She backed away, noting his appraising regard. He reached out and caught her hand in a gentle grasp.

"Easy now. I will not hurt you. I only wish to look upon that arm of yours, it is covered in blood," he said.

"It is not my blood, my lord, it is his." She looked up at him and pointed her finger at Daniel.

"Aye, it is my blood you see upon that witch who meant to rob and kill me!" A soldier was using a strip of cloth to wrap Daniel's wound. His eyes glinted dangerously. "I demand justice, my lord. Release her to my keeping, and I shall see that I have it."

"Nay, my lord!" Her hands reached out to the knight beseechingly. "It is untruths he speaks about me. I did not try to steal from him, and I never intended to harm him."

"What then do you say is the truth?" the knight asked.

Gemma hung her head. She was ashamed and embarrassed to speak of such things in front of anyone, never mind the lord's own men. "He came upon me at his cottage whilst I was preparing his evening meal," she said softly. When the knight appeared to consider her words curiously, she explained. "I came to the village to seek employment, and Daniel...." She paused to look at the man she spoke of. "He took me in, to care for his home and to cook meals for him."

"Go on," the knight pressed.

"Well, as I said, he came upon me whilst I was preparing the evening meal." She hesitated and looked pleadingly up into the knight's face. He regarded her intently, silently commanding her to continue. "He.... Well, that is.... He attacked me, sir," she finished lamely and hung her head again.

His face became stormy. "Do you mean to say the man meant to rape you?"

As Gemma nodded her assent, Daniel leapt toward her threateningly. She cringed, and the knight took up a protective stance before her. Another joined him, his hand gripping the handle of his sword tightly.

"Do not tell me you would believe the word of a whore, my lord," Daniel yelled. "That woman is known throughout the village as a witch and the devil's consort. She has deceived you, just as surely as she deceived me."

"Enough!" the knight commanded. "We will take the girl to Haddon Castle, to my brother, Lord de Bohon. He shall hear the tale, and he will decide what will be done." He then led Gemma to his horse. He mounted and reached down to assist her up.

Gemma looked up at him, and the huge beast he sat upon that was throwing its head about and pawing the ground restlessly. She stared at his outstretched hand in shock. Did he truly mean for her to join him upon his mount? To climb atop that giant animal and ride away with him to Haddon Castle to await judgment? She stole a quick glance at Daniel. He glared at her from behind the man who had stepped forward earlier to stand beside the knight. It would seem she had no choice in the matter. If she were to stay here, Daniel would surely finish what he had started with her. She placed her hand into the knight's and allowed him to pull her up before him. He instructed the others to mount, and they began to ride in the direction of Haddon Castle.

~*~

Tristan was seated upon the dais when Cedric rushed into the great hall. "My lord, my lord! I have returned from the village, and I bring you much news."

"Do not tell me there was trouble again with the villagers." Tristan regarded his bailiff with disbelief as the man hurried toward him. The first patrol of his soldiers had returned saying all had been well within the village.

"Nay, my lord, it is not trouble with the rents I speak of. It is that which happened after a deal was struck with the peasants." Cedric approached the table and poured himself a cup of ale, drinking back a few gulps before continuing his tale. "As the men, your brothers, and I were returning to the castle, we came upon a bloodied pair of peasants fighting on the road."

"Bloodied? What were the louts fighting about?" Tristan asked, his curiosity heightened.

"Not louts, my lord, but a man and a woman." Cedric nodded his head at Tristan's astonished look. "Aye, it seems the man had returned early from the fields and found the wench stealing from him. When he tried to stop her, she pulled forth a dirk and stabbed the poor fellow."

Tristan was stunned. "Stabbed him?"

"Aye, lord. Though the girl says the man is lying, that he came home early and attacked her."

"Why on earth would the man attack her if she was in his own home? Surely they must be a couple then," Tristan asked, confused.

"Nay, she says she only worked for the man."

"Ah, so she works for the man and claims he came home early and attacked her, so she stabbed him with her dirk," he concluded, the story finally making sense to him. "Well, go on then. What did you do?"

"Do, my lord?"

"Aye, what did you do with the quarreling pair?" Tristan asked.

"Oh, this is the strange part, lord. You see, Giles stepped forth to question them both, and when they each gave him their stories, he could not tell which one was truthful, so he decided to bring the girl to you. He would have you decide what to do with her, my lord."

"And what, pray tell, is so strange about that, Cedric?" His patience was beginning to thin.

"Well, the girl, my lord. It seems she has disappeared."

"Disappeared! How could she disappear?"

Cedric took a step back from the dais at Tristan's angry outburst. "Giles had the girl upon his mount, lord. And somewhere between the village and the castle, the girl made her escape."

"And just where are Giles and Denton right now, Cedric, and my soldiers?"

"Why, out searching the forest for the girl, my lord."

"Thad!" Tristan bellowed as he rose to his feet. His squire came barreling into the great hall at the sound of his master's yell. Tristan strode toward the door and headed off to the yard, barking orders at his squire along the way to saddle his mount.

Cedric was close behind him. "My lord, do you mean to ride out to find the men?"

"Aye. I cannot have my men trudging about the forest searching for some foolish girl."

Tristan paced in front of the stables until Thad and a nervous groom brought out his horse. As the two young men held tight to the ill-tempered beast, he yanked on his gloves. He made a quick check of the sword at his side and bent to feel for the dagger he kept tucked into his boot. Satisfied he was well armed, he mounted his horse and swung the animal around to ride toward the gatehouse. The guards hastened to crank the chain that would lift the portcullis.

As the sun began to sink into the horizon, and darkness began to claim the land, Tristan rode off to search for his brothers and his men.

~*~

While the men diligently searched the surrounding area for her, Gemma sat motionless. After making an excuse of needing to attend to her needs, she had run off at breakneck speed in the direction of her cottage. She managed to get a far distance, but knew scampering around would no doubt draw attention to herself, so she had found a small alcove and hidden within. She sat still for what felt like hours before the men gave up their search of the woods and returned to the roadway. Stealthily she rose and began to venture farther into the thick trees.

When she finally reached the safety of her cottage, she removed the torn and bloodied gown she wore and donned another that she retrieved from her trunk. She paced around the little cabin, restlessly, trying to calm herself. What would she do now? There was no doubt in her mind that the lord's men would continue to search for her until she had been brought to justice. They must now believe her guilty of the crimes she was accused of, perceiving her flight proof of her misdeeds. She had foolishly sealed her own fate. But she could not allow herself to be brought forth to the castle, feeling certain the lord would never believe her tale. Returning to the village was out of the question. They would surely hand her over to Lord de Bohon — or worse. Without the aid of the villagers and with winter fast approaching, she would surely perish. Frustrated, she fled the cottage to seek the comfort of the standing stones.

She crept up the slight hill and leaned her aching body against one of the formations. Eyes closed, she wrapped her arms around herself. The night air was becoming cooler, as darkness had now settled upon the land, and the slight breeze in the air brushed upon the dampness of her skin. She had left her cloak at Daniel's cottage, and cursed herself for a fool — how could she reclaim it now? Her satchel and dagger had also been abandoned in her haste. It hurt to lose her meager possessions, but there was naught else she could have done.

Wiping frustrated tears from her eyes, she rose and began to pace between the stones. How could Daniel have done this to her? Why would he attack her like that, and then lie to the villagers and the soldiers about what had happened? *To save his own sorry skin,* she bitterly answered herself. What a fool she'd been to believe things would be well. She should have never trusted Daniel — she should have never gone to the village for aid.

She stood in the middle of the stones and raised her arms over her head. She tilted her head back and began to whisper an ancient chant, moving her hips in rhythm to her words. As her voice grew stronger and louder, she swayed. She knew not where the words and movements came from, except that they were a part of her, always deep in her mind and soul. Her heritage, her birthright. She claimed them now.

She danced, turning around in circles, her arms reaching out to the heavens as her hair flew wildly around her. The wind began to howl, and the leaves joined in the dance, swirling about her slim ankles. Lightning cracked, lighting up the skies and the forest. She was oblivious to the chaos beginning above and around her. Thunder rolled, and lightning again lit up the land, casting an eerie glow upon the stones. And as she danced her fury and her regret to the skies, she slowly became aware she was no longer alone.

A lone warrior and his destrier stood beyond the slope of the hill. Blanketed within the darkness, like an apparition, he had appeared. His gaze focused upon her.

The man who had haunted her nights. The man who had pervaded her dreams.

Now, as Gemma became silent and still, she knew...he had come for her.

CHAPTER 3

It was a time of reckoning—a time for dreams to become reality.

Gemma stood rigid upon the hill, waiting for the warrior to come for her. She knew not what he was, be he man or apparition or demon, but she knew he had come to claim her. Breaking through the boundary of sleep, he had found her.

As she watched, it was like her dream unfolding before her eyes. The beast began to thunder towards her. The ground shook from the pounding of massive hooves upon the hill. She felt her knees give way to terror as she dropped down and stared, frightened and captivated by the scene before her. Closer and closer, he came until he was almost atop her. She bent low and covered her head with her arms protectively, awaiting the assault she was sure to come.

But like her dream, the attack never came.

She opened her eyes and placed her hands upon the ground before her. Bare inches away from her, the animal had stopped. And there it remained.

As her eyes trailed slowly up the length of the horse, her gaze finally came to rest upon the warrior. He sat upon the great beast as if he were carved from stone, so still was he.

In her dream, the warrior had worn a helm, its visor shielding his eyes from view. This man's head was not covered. Instead, he was crowned with a glorious mane of blond hair that the wind whipped wildly about his head. His eyes were piercing, and even with the darkened sky, she could feel the ice in his blue-eyed stare. Unlike in her dream, she had no wish to speak with this man. Her endless list of questions had all but fled her mind, for this was no dream—nay, it was a living nightmare.

His hardened stare held her captive as she slowly rose, and they engaged in a silent struggle of wills. He had come to take her to Haddon, she realized. That was why he was here. She looked briefly away, her gaze straying over his broad shoulders as lightning again flashed. The approaching storm would soon be upon them.

He tilted his head to peer into the raging sky, then motioned for her to come to him.

She regarded him fearfully and began to back away. Before he suspected anything, she spun around and tore away. Down the hill, past the circle of stones, she fled. She was entering the woods when she heard him urge his horse in her direction. She zigzagged and leapt over obstacles in her path, trying to put as much distance between them as possible. But try as she might, she could not elude the warrior and his cursed animal.

She was tiring. As she slowed, frightening thoughts began to seize her. What did this man want of her? Images of what she had endured at Daniel's hands made her shudder in dread. Would he take her, here upon the forest floor, and mayhap kill her afterward? Her feet stilled, but her heart raced on as she leaned against a tree to catch her breath.

Rain began to drop from the skies as thunder rumbled in the distance. She lifted her face to feel the cool dampness and froze as she heard a snap of a branch. Fear crept throughout her veins, her instincts telling her she was no longer alone. Unfortunately, she had lost the game. Before her, emerging from behind the brush, came the warrior. He was not pleased.

She watched as he dismounted and marched forward to tower over her. Straight and brave, she stood. Though she had lost the race, she would be no cowering prisoner. The rain was coming down faster now, causing the thin fabric of her dress to cling to her curves. He stared at her like a wolf about to devour its prey, and she tried not to shake with apprehension. Hardening her gaze, she attempted to appear defiant, not wanting to show him her fear. He reached out, taking hold of her arm lest she try to escape him again.

"Do not attempt to flee, girl. You have wasted enough of my time and that of my soldiers." He dragged her towards his horse and proceeded to grasp her around the waist and toss her into the saddle.

Gemma gave a startled gasp at his rough handling. She contemplated jumping from the animal and running off again, but had no time to act before he swung up onto the saddle behind her. Wrapping his strong arm tightly around her waist, he urged the horse on through the forest.

What he had said, shocked her. This was no man of her dreams or some terrible demon come to whisk her away. He was the conqueror of Haddon Castle, Tristan de Bohon, her lord.

His arm held her securely, and as they broke through the forest and followed the road to his castle, she knew she was well and truly caught. What would happen to her once they reached their destination? Would he cast her into his dungeon? Have her whipped, or mayhap even hanged?

She stiffened as he pulled her tighter to him. Did he think she meant to escape him, to further inflame his wrath? Did he think her a fool or a simpleton? Or was he simply inflicting his lust upon her? She straightened her spine and tried to move forward on the saddle, but the arm about her waist only tightened further. It would seem the leopard had her firmly in his claws and was not eager to let her go.

Mist covered the land when Haddon came into view, making the castle appear to be floating above the ground. Gemma had never ventured too close, but now it seemed she was at last fated to enter the fortress, and perhaps never to leave its sturdy walls. Haddon had always been like an imposing giant keeping watch over the lands. The sight of it sent a chill through her.

Lord Tristan led his horse to the outer wall and shouted to the guards in the watchtower to raise the portcullis. The men hastened to obey, no doubt noting the anger in their lord's voice.

As they rode through the yard, a pair of young lads hurried over to them. Their eager pace slowed when they were close enough to notice their lord was not alone.

Lord Tristan dismounted and tossed the reins to the stable lad, directing him to thoroughly rub down his horse—the animal was as sodden as his master. Then he reached up and grasped her hips, swinging her down to the ground before him. The two lads stared at her with apprehension, then quickly went about their task. Lord Tristan took hold of her arm and pulled her along with him, her small strides stumbling to keep up as he headed for the castle.

Yanking open the heavy double doors, he entered within, pulling her along. He turned and slammed the doors shut, the loud bang echoing throughout the walls of the stone keep. The noise alerted those within that their lord had returned. Soon the entranceway was alive with activity as the men from the great hall rushed out to see him and his captive.

A young knight was the first to reach his side, and he excitedly questioned him. "We knew you would capture the wench, Tristan! Where did you find her?"

Before he could reply, the knight that had held her in his saddle earlier pushed his way through the curious crowd and approached. "I am glad to see you have been successful where I had failed, brother."

Lord Tristan thumped him on his back. "Fret not, Giles, all is well. I found her amongst the great stones before she too escaped me, but I did not lose sight of her and soon had her within my grasp."

While the men around them laughed, Gemma wished she could disappear between the cracks of the stone floor, so great was her discomfort. Never before had she been within a circle of such a loud and boisterous group. She was mortified to be regarded as a prize that their mighty lord had apprehended.

She felt her fear give way to anger as the rowdy group headed back into the great hall to celebrate their lord's triumph. Again she found herself yanked along like a disobedient child in Lord Tristan's firm grasp as he strode toward the dais.

Stubbornly she rooted her feet to the floor and tugged her arm free of his restraint. He halted immediately and turned his hardened stare upon her. She took a step back and then retreated a few more.

He advanced upon her. "Attempting to flee from me again, are you? Have you not yet learned your lesson that I am not so easily deterred?" His blue eyes glinted with challenge.

"My lord, I only wish to end this game and have my fate known to me," she said, noting they were drawing curious stares from the others.

"What is your name?"

"Gemma, my lord."

"Tis late, Gemma, and we are both soaked through from the storm. I will have your story from you on the morrow, for I would enjoy a heated bath now. I presume you would wish the same?"

She was taken aback by his magnanimous offer. It took her a moment to voice her agreement. "Aye, my lord, you are most generous." She inclined her head towards him.

"Then, I shall bid you be my guest this eve, and I will instruct a servant to show you to a chamber for your use." He gestured to an old woman that stood nearby.

"Aye, my lord?" the woman asked, approaching the pair.

"Hazel, this is Gemma, she will be our guest this eve. Show her to a vacant room upstairs, and send some lads to fetch a tub and some heated water. I will require the same in my room."

"Aye, my lord, at once." Hazel turned her humbled look upon Gemma. "Miss, if ye would please come with me, I shall show ye to your room."

Gemma began to follow the old woman from the hall, then paused to turned toward Lord Tristan. "I bid you good eve, my lord."

"And I you."

She walked through the hall to catch up with Hazel, forcing her steps to remain unhurried. She held her head high, well aware of the men's stares and comments as she passed. By the time she joined Hazel at the foot of the stairs, her face was heated by her discomfort. With the courtesy her lord had shown her, had he marked her as something more to him than just his captive? Hazel was leading the way up the stairs and down a hallway as she contemplated her situation.

"Through here, miss."

Hazel swung open a door and stood aside to allow Gemma to enter within. Hazel followed and knelt before the hearth to set tinder to the wood. Soon flames sparked, and the air grew warm and cozy.

Gemma looked about the small but tidy chamber and found it well to her liking. The bed in the center of the floor took up most of the space. A chest sat at the base of the bed, and a little table rested to the side with a candle placed upon it. There were two shuttered windows on either side of the bed, and a privy screen placed in the corner. A chair beneath one of the windows completed the furnishings.

Hazel rose, satisfied the fire was well fed and turned to her. "I will have the lads bring in the tub now, miss, and I shall bring ye a few sheets for drying."

"Thank you, you are very kind."

Hazel nodded briskly and left the room. Gemma walked over to one of the windows. She unlatched the shutter and swung it open. Bracing her hands upon the sill, she leaned forward to peer through the mist to the land far beneath her. Unmindful of the rain, she was curious to see the view. Just barely could she make out where the edge of the forest began. If only she could climb down the stone walls and escape to the woods, she thought wistfully. But alas, Lord Tristan had chosen her chamber wisely. He must have had her thoughts in mind — the room was on the second floor, too high to safely jump from. At least this room was preferable to the dungeon.

She closed and latched the shutter. Hearing a quick rap upon the door, she opened it and allowed the lads to enter with the wooden tub. They set it before the hearth and left the room to fetch buckets of heating water from the kitchen. When they had nearly completed the task of filling the tub, Hazel entered carrying sheets and a small cake of soap. She also had with her a tray with some bread and cheese. After placing everything on the bed, she asked Gemma if she would require any assistance in disrobing or bathing.

"Nay, Hazel. I can manage on my own, thank you."

"As ye wish, miss. The lads will return to empty and remove the tub when ye are finished."

"Good eve to you then."

"Good eve, miss." Hazel left the room, closing the door behind her.

Gemma stripped off her drenched gown and shift and laid them out over the chair she had placed by the fire. Picking up the soap, she climbed into the tub and sunk into the heated water up to her chin. Her knees bent toward her breasts in the small enclosure. *This is heavenly*, she thought. The only baths she'd ever taken were in the small stream by her cottage. With soap smelling like lavender, she washed her hair and soaped her body, relishing the sweet aroma. When she was finished, she wrapped herself in one of the sheets Hazel had brought her.

Sitting by the fire, she ate the food from the tray while the heat of the flames dried her hair. The lads soon came to take the tub away, and she did not linger long before deciding to go to bed. Exhausted, she donned her now dry shift and crawled beneath the warm blankets on the bed. The bed felt as good as the bath. She sunk deep into the mattress and was quickly asleep.

Her hands and feet were bound tightly to a stake. She looked below and was horrified to see she stood atop a large pile of sticks. The glare from torches cast the faces around her into a hideous light. Laughter sprang from the crowd taking delight in the nightmare in which she found herself.

"Burn the witch!" they cried as she struggled vainly against the ropes that held her captive.

"Nay!" she screamed. "I am not a witch!"

The group of riotous peasants began to hurl their torches upon the mound as she watched helplessly. The timber alit quickly, and she soon felt the heat against her bare feet as the fire danced dangerously close to her skirts.

Then, like an avenging angel riding his war-horse through the mist, a warrior charged toward her. The group of peasants scattered and fled, unwilling to face his wrath. The warrior jumped from his horse and ran toward the fire. He leapt through the flames, unmindful of the peril. After cutting the ropes with his dagger, he lifted her into his strong arms and gave a mighty jump overtop the flames. He lay her down upon the cool grass and leaned over her, concern in his eyes. Then he slowly lowered his head to taste her lips. He was gentle at first, then became more insistent until finally, she felt as though she were being devoured. The warrior broke the passionate kiss and held her close in his arms, looking deeply into her eyes. She stared at the man before her — her champion — and was stunned to discover it was he, her lord, Tristan.

Gemma woke with a start and sat upright in bed, breathing heavily as the remnants of her dream began to slip away. *It cannot be!* The man she had dreamt of for so many nights, the warrior of her dreams, could not be Lord Tristan! She lay back down as she tried to steady her breathing. *Nay,* she thought, *I will fall back to sleep and forget about this. My foolish mind is playing tricks on me.* But sleep eluded her. Every time she closed her eyes, she saw the flames leaping before her face, heard the cruel taunts of the peasants. And Lord Tristan, riding toward her, leaping through the fire to save her. Worst of all was the memory of his lustful kiss upon her lips.

~*~

"My lord, my lord!" yelled Thad early the next morning as he gave one swift knock on Tristan's bedchamber door and rushed inside, unannounced.

Tristan stood before the table in his room, leaning over a bowl, shaving. He reached for a cloth and scrubbed at his face, annoyed at the intrusion. "What is it, lad?"

"Come quickly, my lord, to the stables. 'Tis Fury. He's not well!" The boy was clearly fearful.

Tristan finished dressing and hurried down to the stables to see for himself the state of his prized animal.

The head groom and a stable boy were standing outside of Fury's stall. They looked anxiously toward Tristan as he rushed into the stables, with Thad close on his heels. Tristan strode over to the stall and looked within. His beautiful horse had a slight sheen to his coat, as though he'd recently been ridden hard. Fury's large head hung low, and his legs were shaking. Tristan unlatched the stall and went in. He ran his hands gently over Fury's slick coat, speaking low, soothing words to him.

He turned his face toward the groom. "What ails him, Nathan? He feels hot with fever."

"Aye, my lord. He was fine last night after Thad brought him in and rubbed him down. But toward the middle of the night, he became restless, waking me from a sound sleep. I have seen the like before," he added, casting his gaze toward the suffering animal. "Many years ago, before I come to serve ye, my lord, I worked as a stable hand in Salisbury. The baron there had a highly prized destrier, much like your Fury. One night it developed a malady, much the same as this one." Nathan inclined his head towards Fury. "The man was beside himself in grief and worry, for no one was able to cure the animal. The baron sent forth his men with word of offering a gold coin as reward for a successful cure. Many came forward to offer aid, as the baron's reward was high, but alas, none had any effect. Until one day, an old woman came to offer her services. She called herself a healer, but it was much rumored she was a witch. She made up a potion for the animal and fed it to him many times. Within the week, the animal was much improved. Soon, it was completely recovered." When he finished his story, he looked at Tristan for a reaction.

"Are you telling me a witch cured the baron's horse?" Tristan exclaimed in disbelief.

"Nay, my lord, it was not a witch, but a healer. And aye, she did heal the animal. I saw it with my own eyes."

"Well then, that's it. I will send forth some of my men to find a healer." He lovingly stroked Fury's slick coat. "Rest easy, my beauty, soon you will be well."

~*~

Gemma awoke at dawn, got dressed in her dried gown, and opened the windows in her room, letting in the morning light. Only small puddles remained of the storm's frenzy the previous night. Gazing about the land for a spell, she sat upon the bed anxiously awaiting the summons she knew would come. She pondered her plea to Lord Tristan. It was true she had slashed Daniel with her dagger, but it had been in self-defense. Too, she had fled from his brothers and his men, but she hoped she could convince him she had been in shock over her ordeal and not thinking clearly. Surely the lord would give credit to her tale. He must, for her fate rested upon his belief in her. Without it, she was surely lost. She rose to pace the small room as the morning drew on. Sounds of the castle bustling with activity reached her ears as inhabitants rose, breaking their fast and beginning morning tasks.

There was a soft rap upon her door, and Hazel entered, bearing a tray laden with fresh bread, cheese, and fruit. Gemma accepted it gratefully and placed the tray on the chair. As Hazel turned to leave, Gemma asked, "Pardon, Hazel, but has Lord Tristan asked to have me brought forth to him this morn?"

Hazel turned and had sadness in her smile. "I am afraid not, miss. The lord has much on his mind this morn."

"Is something wrong?"

"Oh, miss, it is not my place to speak of it. I am sure the lord will seek ye out soon." And after saying that, Hazel quickly left the room, leaving Gemma to wonder what was taking place below.

Gemma stood by the window and watched the sun climb as the morning sped by. Lord Tristan still had not summoned her, and she grew anxious. She walked to the chamber door and carefully eased it open, expecting to see a guard posted nearby. The hall was vacant. Cautiously creeping out, she edged down the hall towards the main stairway. At any moment, she feared the hue and cry would sound, but only silence greeted her. Pausing at the top of the stairs, she looked below towards the entrance of Haddon Castle. If only she could make it to the door, then perhaps she could escape. But first, she would have to get past the doorway of the great hall. Stealthily she crept downward, then, reaching the base of the stairway, she began to walk steadily towards the front doors. As she neared the great hall, she could hear voices within. There was no other choice except to make a run for it, hoping no one would notice her. After a deep breath, she made a dash towards the doors. A shout to "halt" came from the great hall. Someone had seen her, but she was already at the doors and was not about to give up so easily. Not when freedom was within her grasp.

She grappled with the door, trying vainly to push it open, but it was heavy and unwilling to give way. Just as the sound of pounding feet gained proximity, the door miraculously flew open. Fleeing the impending approach of the men behind her, she rushed outside — only to run straight into the huge chest of Lord Tristan.

"By God, Gemma. What is going on here? Where are you rushing off to in such a hurry?" Lord Tristan stood formidable and dangerously still, glaring down upon her from his great height. His piercing gaze shifted to the men who had run up behind her.

"She was trying to escape, my lord!" said one of them.

Lord Tristan looked down at her flushed and guilty face. "I thought we settled this last eve, Gemma. If you run, I shall find you. You cannot escape me."

"Aye, my lord. I know it well. It is just that I have wondered what was going on below. I have waited for you to send for me and you have not. Hazel mentioned that other matters required your attention."

"So you just decided to leave, then?"

"Forgive me, my lord, but there are matters I myself must tend to."

"What *matters* do you speak of that are so important you must rush away?"

"Well...." She kept her head lowered as she answered. "I require more healing plants, my lord. The season has not been good for growing, and I must find what I can whilst the weather is fair."

"Healing plants? What do you do with them?"

"I use them to ease the suffering of the villagers when they are ailing or hurt, my lord." Although, she thought, it would most likely not be any time soon that the villagers would call upon her after Daniel had spread his vicious lies. She lifted her head to await the scorn she was sure would come when he discovered her to be the "witch of the forest."

"You are a healer?"

"Aye, my lord, I am," she said hesitantly, being caught off guard from the sudden change in his visage. Mercy, she thought, he almost looked to be excited.

"Good," he said, as he grasped her arm and began to lead her outside and in the direction of the stables. "I have need of a healer, urgently."

As he maintained a steady pace towards his destination, she tried to hurry her steps to keep up with him. When they reached the stable, he flung open the doors and urged her inside.

"My lord, is someone ill or hurt? Is it your groom or one of the stable boys?" she inquired, searching around the dim interior for the patient.

He pulled her over to one of the stalls and waved his hand within. She gasped as she looked into the stall and saw none other than his prized destrier. The beast that had relentlessly pursued her through the forest.

CHAPTER 4

"Tell me you can help him." Tristan's look was hopeful and expectant as he regarded her.

She lowered her eyes as she answered him. "Nay, I cannot tell you that, my lord."

He reached out to grasp her arms. "What do you mean? You told me you are a healer."

"Please, my lord." She tried to free herself, only to find her arms held tighter.

Tristan pulled her up tight against his chest and leaned his face close to her. "Hear me and hear me well. You *will* tend my horse, and you *will* make him well again." He abruptly released her, causing her to stumble back a few steps.

She lifted her head to glare at him. "You mistake my words, my lord." She attempted to keep the ire from her voice. "I have not said I would not help. 'Tis only that I cannot assure you of success."

"Do what you can, it is all I ask." Hope returned to his face.

"Aye, I shall. But first, I will need to gather the healing plants I require."

"I will escort you myself."

It was clear he did not trust her to go off on her own. "I will require a satchel, or a basket to collect the plants. Then I must have use of your kitchen or a spare room so I may prepare a tonic." She spoke as she looked into Fury's stall and tentatively reached her hand toward the animal, stroking his neck, feeling the heat of the fever in him. "What is his name?"

"Fury."

"Well...." She started towards the stable door. "Shall we begin?"

Tristan strode through the yard as she hurried to keep pace with him. As they walked towards the doors of Haddon, Thad rushed up to them. "My lord, have ye need of me?"

"Aye lad, run to the kitchen and fetch me a basket or such, something to gather plants in." He turned to Gemma after Thad ran off to do his bidding. "What plants do you need?"

She thought for a moment. "I will need to gather yarrow plant, and mayhap some meadowsweet to treat the fever. We will need to fast him and keep his bowels open while we dose him with a potion to promote sweating to cool his temperature."

Lord Tristan took note of the sudden frown upon her face. "What is it?"

"Oh, it is naught. I just remembered I had collected some yarrow plant yesterday. In my haste to leave the village, my satchel was left behind," she said quietly, reflecting upon the sorry events leading to her present situation. She looked up at him and wondered if he may now take the time to question her about Daniel. He seemed about to do just that when Thad breathlessly rejoined them, waving a basket in his hand.

She took the basket from the boy and looked at Lord Tristan expectantly. "Shall we be off, my lord?"

"Aye, let us go."

As Gemma walked, thoughts entered her head. If she were successful in healing Fury, would Lord Tristan allow her to leave unchallenged? Or would he still question her as to what took place with Daniel? And if so, would he believe her tale, or would he decide she was guilty of an attempt of theft and murder? What would her punishment be if it were so? She shuddered involuntarily, for she well knew Lord Tristan's justice would be swift and undoubtedly ruthless.

~*~

Tristan's gaze continuously strayed to Gemma as the pair trudged through the forest, eyes focused on the ground. She had pushed up the sleeves of her gown, and every few steps she would drop to her knees to inspect a plant she saw. He walked up behind her and peered over her shoulders, his eyes straying to the front of her gown, which offered up a delightful view.

Seeming oblivious to him, she gently snapped off a plant at its base and carefully laid it in the basket. She rose, and he backed away from her, his face feeling slightly flushed. She lifted the basket and continued to search about the forest for more plants, unaware of his sudden discomfort.

Tristan watched a play of emotions cross Gemma's face, and had no doubt as to what she thought. He had not summoned her this morn to hear her story about last eve's events, and he knew she must be expecting him to ask for her defense. He would get the tale from her soon, but for now, he let his thoughts stray....

Last night had seemed like some sort of strange dream. The lightning crashing angrily around him, and Gemma dancing beneath the sky, singing out to the heavens, reaching out to him like an enchantress. How had he known to find her there? It was as though some unseen force had led him to her, but for what purpose? She was nothing to him. He had not cared too greatly whether he had returned to Haddon without her.

Or did he care?

Something about her intrigued him when he had seen her. So defiant, so angry. So beautiful and desirable. When she had fled, he had felt himself denied — of what he knew not. Only that he had been overwhelmed by a fierceness deep within him to hunt her down and claim her for his own. When he had captured her, he'd had to fight the lust within himself and remember that he was Lord of Haddon, and the girl was under his protection. Little had she known it was he she needed to be protected from.

Tristan noticed a small stream nearby and headed over to it. He knelt to drink and then called to Gemma to come and join him. She hesitantly walked over to him, her weary look relaying her thoughts. He watched her kneel and drink deeply from her cupped hands. He noted how tired she appeared, and surmised fear had most likely led to a restless night for her. The morning had been long and overly warm. He cursed himself and his impetuous departure from the castle without thought of food or drink to sustain them.

"I believe we have gathered enough plants to tend to Fury, my lord," she told him.

"That is good. The day marches on, and I would have him

tended with due haste." He stood and reached out his hand to assist her in rising.

~*~

Gemma looked up at him and noted how huge and strong he was. It was no wonder he was thought of throughout the land as Edward's champion, for his look was that of a fierce, undefeated warrior. The blond mane on his head, shone in the sunlight and brushed lightly upon his powerful shoulders. His blue eyes were sharp and piercing, showing keen intelligence. Lord Tristan's arms were bare, and sun bronzed, no doubt from many days spent in the yard at swordplay. His legs were long, and hard muscles strained against the breeches that held them. As he looked at her, awaiting her hand, his lips quirked a bit as though he would offer a smile. Or he had noticed her assessment of him and found it amusing. She put her small hand into his much larger one and felt herself slowly lifted to her feet. His grasp was warm and strong, and she felt a jolt of something unusual go through her body.

He held fast to her and seemed loath to let her go — he too must have felt the sensation their touch created. Recovering herself quickly, she went to pull away, but as she turned, she felt his grip upon her hand hold fast. She peered back at him questioningly and was shocked to discover the heat in his stare. Fear washed over her — she had seen that look before.

"My lord, if you wish to tend Fury, then we best be about it." She jerked her hand abruptly from his and met his heated gaze with a fiery one.

"Aye, that we should." He looked at her a moment longer before stalking off through the woods with determined strides.

Gemma worked diligently throughout the afternoon, preparing a tonic she would administer to Fury. She had secured a small workroom near the kitchen of the castle and had brought her plants within. With all her thoughts focused on the task at hand, she had not given herself time to reflect upon what had taken place with Lord Tristan in the forest. As the light through the window of the small room began to dim, she realized the hour was growing late. Hazel had brought her a tray from the kitchen for the evening meal, but it remained untouched upon the table where it had been placed. Finally satisfied her work was complete, she reached for the tray and drank some ale to quench her thirst. She wearily took a seat upon a chair set at the table and began to partake of the food before her.

Her thoughts now turned to Lord Tristan, and she was troubled by what had transpired between them. She could not deny the feelings that had coursed through her body with his touch. And the way he had looked at her....

Abruptly she rose from the chair, her hunger forgotten. She reached for the tonic she'd made and headed out of the room. The sooner she healed Fury, the sooner she could leave this cursed place. She hoped.

~*~

Tristan was in the stables leaning against Fury's stall as Nathan approached. After seeing Gemma settled in, he had come and kept silent vigil over the animal.

"Any change, my lord?" Nathan asked.

"Nay, I am afraid not. He seems to be growing weaker and more fevered."

Suddenly the stable door swung open, and Gemma

hurried in. Tristan immediately became alert and watched her anxiously as she approached, carrying the tonic.

"Is it ready?"

"Aye, my lord." She looked at Nathan. "Hello, I am Gemma. What is your name?"

"Nathan, miss."

"Nathan, I will require some assistance with the animal. Will you aid me?"

"Aye, miss, be happy to."

"I will aid you, Gemma," Tristan said, stepping forward.

"Surely, there are duties that require your attention elsewhere, my lord?"

"Nay, none that are more important than this." He could sense her unease.

"As you wish." She turned to Nathan. "I will require two buckets, one of them filled with water, please." He went off to fetch them, and when he returned, Gemma took out the tonic and poured it into the empty bucket before adding a bit of water to it. "He has fasted today?"

"Aye, miss."

"Good, then he should be ready for a drink of this sweet potion." She walked over and handed the bucket to Tristan. "Give it to him, my lord. It will help bring down his fever."

He took the bucket and placed it in Fury's stall. As the animal drank, Tristan turned to her. "What is next?"

"Now I will add some dried herb to the water, and we shall bathe him with it. This, too, shall help relieve the fever."

She emptied the herbs into the bucket and asked Nathan for any rags he may have about. He searched around the stable and returned with a handful. Gemma soaked them in the water, then brought the bucket over to Fury's stall and gave it to Tristan. The three of them took turns bathing the animal as the evening wore on. Few words were spoken throughout the long night, all of them focused on the task before them.

When morning finally arrived, the birds sang as they circled the high towers of Haddon, welcoming the day. Tristan emerged from the stables, shading his eyes from the bright sunlight, a smile on his weary face.

Thad was the first to run up to him. "My lord, is Fury well?"

"It is too soon to tell yet, lad, but aye, he is much improved," he said as he walked through the yard. Their actions last night had met with a good degree of success. He was hopeful but was also very much in need of some rest. He had bid Nathan and Gemma to take their ease as well, but both had preferred to remain in the stables to be close by Fury if need be.

He, however, much desired the comfort of his own chamber. Not just for the soft bed, but after spending the night so closely with Gemma, he felt the need to place himself at a distance from her. She not only had earned his respect last night, but he was experiencing other feelings, ones that would no doubt shock her if she had known.

He finally entered his chamber, stripped off his clothing, and lay down on his bed to sleep. As he drifted off, he assured himself that it was only gratitude he felt for the girl. Of course, he also was enchanted by her beauty, for he was a man, but surely that was all he felt for her.

~*~

Gemma continued to remain alert and watchful of her charge.

"Gemma." Nathan approached her and talked quietly. "I will send for Thad and some stable lads to watch over Fury for a spell. Seek your ease, for ye are surely in need of some rest."

She rubbed a hand over her tired eyes and noted Nathan's fatigued expression. No doubt she could use a few hours to rest and mayhap have a little food, as surely the danger had now passed. She took a last look at Fury, and satisfied he appeared much improved, she decided she too would take her leave.

"Nathan, I thank you for your aid. You are right that I am tired. I will seek my bed, and I bid you do the same."

"Aye, miss, I believe I shall."

She shielded her eyes from the sudden glare of light as she stepped out of the dim stables. Walking to the doors of Haddon, she noted as she crossed the yard that it was streaming with workers and soldiers. She looked over her shoulder toward the outer wall's gate and noted hopelessly how well guarded it was. There was no other choice but to enter the castle, as escape would prove impossible with so many watchful eyes upon her. A guard at the heavy wooden doors allowed her entry, and she walked in and headed past the great hall to the kitchen. Perhaps the cook would allow her a bit of bread and cheese as she, Nathan, and Lord Tristan had missed the morning meal. Lord Tristan had made it clear the night before that they were not to be disturbed. No doubt, a tray would have been prepared and sent up to the lord's room upon his return. She did not expect the same consideration would be given to her.

The castle was quiet, as most of the inhabitants were

outside while the weather proved fair. There was still much work to be done in preparation for the winter months. She entered the kitchen and found a few women busy cleaning up from the morning meal. As she walked within, the cook took note of her and quickly ushered her over to the table and placed cheese and bread before her. As she handed her a cup of ale, she regarded her curiously.

"'Ave we met before, miss?"

Gemma looked up from the tray to the older woman, who was watching her with interest. "Nay, I think not. I have never been to the castle before. I live outside the walls of Haddon in the forest near the village."

"Ye 'ave a familiar look 'bout ye, miss," the cook insisted.

"Well, you are mistaken. I am sure we have not met before."

"Hmm," the woman replied and left with a shake of her head.

Gemma finished her meal and left the kitchen to head up the stairway to her chamber. Reaching the landing on the second floor, she turned to the left and walked slowly down the corridor toward her room. There were many doors along the hall, and as she passed them, she wondered if Lord Tristan might be behind one of them. Pushing all thoughts of him from her head, she paused as one of the doors ahead of her cracked open slightly, and she heard a "Psst."

She halted and looked at the darkened entrance of the room. Then she heard it again. Being the only person in the corridor, there was no doubt whoever was behind the door, they were beckoning her. She approached the room cautiously, and as she neared, the door opened slightly more. A wrinkled face peered out at her with dull brown eyes and a wide smile.

"Lady, please come within, for I must speak with ye," the old woman said in a hushed whisper.

Gemma only hesitated briefly before she joined the mysterious stranger in the room. "What is it you wish of me, madam?" She realized she, too, was whispering.

The old woman shut the door after peering down the corridor. Gemma looked around, noticing how much more spacious and furnished the room was than her own. As she took in the huge four-poster bed with a canopy and surrounding thick velvet curtains, she knew this room must belong to the lady of Haddon. She was fearful for a moment that someone may come upon them in the lady's room. Having the suspicion of theft already thrown her way, she had no wish to remain overlong.

The shutters were drawn tight against the sunny day, and as her eyes adjusted to the dimness of the room, she took note of the layers of dust upon the furnishings. This was not a room that had been used in a very long while. She regarded the old woman and noticed she was staring at her as though she were looking at an apparition. She crept up to Gemma, taking in every detail of her appearance, then circled her as she mumbled incoherent words to herself. Finally, she seemed satisfied and halted right in front of her.

Gemma regarded the old woman questioningly, but before she could say a word, the old woman embraced her and proclaimed, "Thank the gods, Lady Talitha's daughter has finally come home!"

Gemma was stunned by the old woman's acclamation. Was she mad, she wondered?

The old woman beheld her, her eyes filling with unshed tears. "All will be well now that ye, my lady, have come to reclaim Haddon as the rightful heir."

"What is your name, madam?" Gemma asked.

"'Tis Adele, my lady, your most humble servant." The old woman sunk into a deep curtsy.

"Please, Adele, do not." She reached over to lightly grasp her arm and raise her up. "I know naught of Lady Talitha, nor of Haddon's heir."

"My lady, ye are the very image of Lady Talitha. Ye must be her lost daughter, finally, come home."

Gemma was stunned. "Adele, why would you think I am heir to Haddon?"

"Why, my lady, I briefly set eyes upon ye when ye first arrived, but I watched from the shadows 'til I was certain. And now that I have seen ye up close, I know it to be true," she said with a quick nod of her head.

"How could you be certain, Adele?" Gemma asked warily.

Adele reached out her hand and placed her fingers lightly upon the torc that encircled Gemma's neck. "'Tis this, my lady. It belonged to Lady Talitha, the Lady of Haddon."

Gemma backed slowly away from Adele. *Nay, it cannot be!* The woman was mistaken. But what if she were not? her mind demanded. For what did she really know of her past? As a small child, she had been abandoned and left for dead at the standing stones. Gran had found her and raised her for the next several years of her life, before sadly passing away. Once she was old enough to ask questions, Gran had told her that her mother had given her the torc. Her mother had worn it before passing it down to Gemma. She had said her ancestors were a proud and powerful tribe of Celtic warriors and Druids and her mother part of a lineage of people who secretly kept the old traditions and religion alive. When she had asked the whereabouts of her mother, Gran would say only that she had gone away and would not return. Although it had saddened her to think of her unknown family, she had accepted what she could not change.

"Tell me of Lady Talitha, Adele," she said with a calm she did not feel.

"She was beautiful, my lady, like ye." Adele had a faraway look in her eyes. "She came to this place a prisoner of the old lord, Edwin Madmont. He had been nigh the border of Wales when he spied her. It was said he was instantly besotted and declared he had to have her for his own. She had been traveling with a small train to be united with her betrothed when Madmont and his men set upon them and killed them all. He stole Lady Talitha and brought her to Haddon, and forcefully wed her."

Adele looked sadly about the room before she continued. Gemma could only stand numbly by and await the rest of the story to be told.

"This was her chamber." Adele waved an aged hand about the room. "She spent most of her time here, hiding away from the drunken rantings of Madmont. Eight months after they were wed, she gave birth to a child, a girl. She was a beautiful, delightful child, filled with laughter and smiles. She was the only joy in my lady's life. Madmont despised the child. He did not believe she was his own. He thought the child to be that of Lady Talitha's betrothed, Lord Tarquin Alexander."

Adele looked at her with such despair that Gemma shook with a sudden chill.

Gemma began to walk slowly around the room, seeing it with new eyes. Had this been her mother's chamber? Was there a chance she could be the child Adele had spoken of? *Nay!* her thoughts rebelled. If it were so, should she not have some memory of this place? A place she had lived at for a time, even briefly? The sight of Haddon Castle had always filled her with an overwhelming sense of dread and fear. But why did she fear this place? Could there be a reason, buried deep within her mind, that she should feel such fear? She remembered naught.

"That night, so long ago, will live with me forever." Adele's eyes appeared dazed, as though some terrible scene replayed in her memory. "I remember being below when I heard my lady's screams. Madmont had drunk himself into an angry, foul temper, and had gone up to Lady Talitha's room. I rushed to her chamber when I heard the lord's mad screams and tried to gain entrance, but the door had been bolted from within. I could hear her crying and begging him not to hurt the child. All I could do was wait for him to leave. Finally, there was silence — terrible, awful silence. Madmont left the chamber, and when I rushed to my lady's side, she was lying on the floor in a pool of her own blood. As I gently raised her head, she fearfully cried, 'My child, my beautiful child, what has he done to her?' I found the child 'cross the room. She lay still upon the floor, barely alive. I lifted her and brought her to her mother." Adele looked at Gemma in anguish.

"Please, Adele, I would hear all of it," she said despondently.

"I could see Lady Talitha was nigh death, but her only concern was for the safety of her daughter. She begged me to hide the child. To take her to the standing stones, where the gods would protect and watch over her. I promised my lady I would do as she asked. Lady Talitha then placed her torc 'bout the child's neck. Finally, able to rest in peace, she passed away. I took the child to the stones. It was easy enough to steal away, for the lord and his guards were well into their cups and took no notice of a servant carrying what they thought was a bundle of sheets. When I laid the child down amongst the stones, I feared she was too far gone to live. But still, I offered up prayers to the gods to help her and keep her safe. Then I returned to the castle. The next morning I came back to see if the child had indeed died in the night, but when I reached the place I had left her, the child was gone. I never knew if she survived or if the wolves had dragged her off into the night. Until now." She looked at Gemma, her eyes shining resolutely.

"I was found at the standing stones when I was a young child," Gemma said quietly. "An old woman I called Gran told me this. She was a healer to the village people but lived alone in the forest. She healed me and raised me as her own child for many years before she died."

"The gods did hear my prayers that night. They sent the old woman to find ye." Adele clapped her hands in glee, then quieted, warily looking about the room.

"But how would she know of the torc, or of my mother's origins?" Gemma asked.

"I do not know, my lady. Since she has now passed, we may never know."

Gemma suddenly felt overwhelmed and exhausted. She had much to consider, but she needed rest to provide her with a clear head to think through all she had learned.

"I am weary, Adele. I have not been to sleep all night. Lord Tristan and his groom and I tended Fury 'til this morning. I was seeking my bed when you summoned me."

"Please, my lady, take your ease, for ye have much to think about and many plans to make."

Adele led her to the door. She peeked her head out into the corridor to make sure it was clear before stepping aside to let her pass.

Gemma began to walk towards her own room further down the corridor before she turned to whisper a quick goodbye to Adele.

"Sleep well, my lady," Adele whispered, then hurried off in the opposite direction.

~*~

Tristan entered the great hall, finding his brothers conversing with some of his soldiers. After sleeping long, he had arisen to find himself feeling refreshed and hungry. He had not bothered with the tray of food left in his room when he retired earlier. Feeling overtired and not fit company after the tiring night he had spent in the stables, he now wished to partake of the evening meal with his compatriots. He looked about the large room, hoping to spy Gemma seated at one of the many tables, but she was not within. He approached Giles and Denton.

"Tristan, 'tis good to see you, brother," said Giles.

"Aye, we have been to the stables to see how Fury fares, and it would seem he is on the mend," Denton added.

"That is good to hear. I have not seen him since this morn." Tristan looked at his youngest brother. "Have you seen Gemma? I wonder if she is still abed or if she has returned to the stables."

"Nay, I have not seen your pretty healer, brother," Denton replied, smiling.

"Nor have I. Would you like a servant sent to her room to see if she still sleeps, Tristan?" Giles asked.

"Aye, for I would have her join us for the evening meal."

Tristan's gaze searched the hall for Hazel. He spotted her near the doorway of the kitchen and gestured to her to come to him. After sending her off to look in on Gemma, he took his seat at the trestle table. A short while later, Gemma entered the great hall. She appeared lost, and a little frightened as all the unfamiliar faces regarded her with curiosity. Tristan stood and called out to her to join him. She approached the table and stood in front of him. He smiled down at her from his great height.

"I hope your rest was pleasant," he said.

"Aye, thank you, my lord."

"I would have you join me for the evening meal, here by my side."

"B...but, my lord, I am only a peasant. It would not be right for me to sit at your side."

"I bid you, please, join me," he invited more loudly. He came around the table and held out his hand for her to take. Hesitantly she allowed him to lead her up to the chair beside his, which Giles had relinquished. He saw her seated, and after taking his own seat, looked around at the others at the table and then in the great hall with a chilling glance, daring any to gainsay him.

Gemma appeared uncomfortable seated above her station between him and Giles. Denton, seated on his other side, offered her a warm smile. The hall was silent as all within openly stared at her. When Tristan signaled the servants to begin serving the meal, the hall began to fill with the sounds of conversation. Gemma seemed grateful for the distraction the food created and looked over at him only to find him staring back at her. They shared a trencher, and he had speared a piece of meat with his dagger and now held it out for her to accept. She bent forward shyly and bit the proffered piece with her teeth.

He smiled as he watched her. The sight of her small, sharp little teeth made him envision her doing things with them other than eating bits of meat. Her tongue darted out and licked the juice from her lips. He had to turn away, the small act so inflamed him with lust.

After the main course of beef seasoned with onions and garlic, peas, and beans cooked in a fish broth, was completed, the servants began to bring out fruit and pastries, along with fresh jugs of wine.

Tristan refilled the goblet they shared and turned to her. "I would like to ask you something, Gemma."

She reached for the goblet and took a large gulp. Tristan watched the expression on her face turn to one of dread. He wondered if she feared he would now begin questioning her about what had happened in the village. He planned to do just that, but he would do so privately. Now he had another thought on his mind.

"I would like for you to remain here at Haddon as the

castle healer." He caught her hand before she could reach for the wine again. "You have shown yourself to have remarkable skill, and it would serve us well to have you here amongst us."

"My lord, I am much flattered by your proposal," she said a little breathlessly, obviously relieved by his offer. She took a few moments before she finally responded. "I gratefully accept your most generous offer, my lord."

Tristan was pleased with her acquiescence. "Good. I shall inform a couple of my men to escort you home to retrieve any clothing or personal belongings. I will also see that a room is set up for your use as Haddon's healer."

"My lord," she said with hesitation. "You are very kind, but I must ask that I be granted a measure of privacy when returning to my cottage. I have lived there all of my life, and I would appreciate a few quiet moments alone to bid farewell to the place."

"Of course. I shall have them escort you just close enough to offer assistance if it is required." *And to make sure that you do not attempt to flee,* he thought silently.

CHAPTER 5

After the evening meal, Lord Tristan accompanied Gemma to the stables, where she administered another dose of the tonic to Fury. It had been fortunate, she told him, that the horse's condition had been noted early and quickly looked after. She felt certain Fury would be well by the week's end. Nathan's presence in the stables had relieved her. She'd been tense when Lord Tristan offered to accompany her, and the thought of spending more time alone with him had set her on edge.

Later, after she retired for the night, she lay awake for hours. Since she had slept most of the day away, she was not feeling very tired. Instead, she contemplated the tale Adele had told her. So many thoughts ran through her mind. It seemed too fantastic to even imagine that she — the witch of the forest — could, in fact, be the daughter of the Lady Talitha of Haddon, and that perchance, Madmont was her sire. She shook with a slight tremor of foreboding. It would be easier to imagine herself the daughter of the Lord Tarquin, who Adele had mentioned. The man had been Talitha's betrothed. Could it be possible they had consummated their union before the actual wedding?

She gave up the pretense of trying to sleep and rose from her bed. She stirred up the fire, bringing bright, high flames to life, and reflected dancing shadows against the walls. On the floor before the hearth, she stared into the flames. If there were a chance Lord Tarquin was her sire, what if she could find the man? Adele had said she greatly resembled Lady Talitha, so there was a possibility he may recognize her. She wondered if Adele knew where Lord Tarquin resided. An hour later, exhaustion began to overtake her. She crawled back into bed and swiftly fell asleep, dreaming sweet dreams of being reunited with a father who much adored her.

~*~

Gemma looked over her shoulder, making sure the guards didn't attempt to follow her as she strolled away from the stream by her cottage. After leading them as close as she felt was a safe enough distance, she had requested they accompany her no further. She had relayed to them that she required a private moment to gather her belongings and bid farewell to the cottage she had grown up in. Although they took their ease by the stream's edge, she could see they remained aware of her every step. There was no doubt their lord had instructed them to be vigilant in their task at guarding her well.

As she approached her small, tidy cottage, she felt a sense of remorse and regret to be leaving her home, her sanctuary. She pushed those thoughts aside as she strode resolutely up the pathway, and thought upon the new life awaiting her at Haddon Castle.

Once inside, she began bundling up her pitiful amount of

clothing into a cloth sack. There was nothing the front room contained that she would require once at the castle. Pots and bowls and cups would be aplenty there, and she wished to leave some items behind, as she may one day have need of them again.

She eyed Gran's chest of clothing and personal items mournfully. It seemed a lifetime ago they had shared laughter and tears in this little hidden cottage deep in the forest. Oh, how she missed the sound of Gran's voice, the sparkle in her eye and her comforting, gentle touch.

She ran her hands lovingly over the worn surface of the chest. This, too, she would leave behind in the privacy and safety of the cottage. Perhaps she would return from time to time, to sit and remember the years past. She lifted the lid of the chest, for within she recalled that Gran had kept a small wooden box containing special mementos collected throughout her long life. There was a small beaded bracelet given to her by a suitor when she was ten and four. It had held fond memories for Gran, and Gemma wished to bring it along so she may have something of Gran's near to her.

She pushed aside some old clothing and worn blankets to locate the box. Finding it, she lifted it out and placed it on the floor. The outside was worn by age and much handling; the lid was decorated with many carvings. The detail of the carvings showed that someone had taken much pride and time to carefully fashion it. On the right side of the lid, almost hidden since it was part of the design, were initials. Two letters that were a mystery to her, as Gran had never told her what they stood for. She ran her finger lightly over the tiny CH. She undid the small catch at the front and lifted the lid to search for the beads.

As she searched about the box with her hand, the bottom of it seemed crooked somehow, as if one side was pushed down farther than the other. She emptied the contents so she may study it more closely. Gemma set aside ribbons and colored feathers, a dainty leather belt, the bracelet she sought, and a small beaded purse, with care. Then she turned the box over and around, and again looked within, suddenly noticing the inside of it was much smaller than the outside. She reached inside and pressed down on the crooked bottom, and felt a small pin placed in the corner to hold it up.

Gemma set the box aside and went into the front room to locate a dagger. She returned and began to pry the bottom from the box. To her surprise, it lifted out with not much effort, and beneath it was a hidden compartment. She was stunned to discover that which lay within, as she lifted out a small book with a worn leather cover. As she leafed through it, she noticed several of the many pages were neatly printed upon, as though it was someone's personal journal. This was indeed a surprise—she had never seen or heard Gran mention this journal. But Gran must have known of its existence, for she had possessed the treasured box for most of her years.

Placing the journal aside, she donned the beaded bracelet and replaced the makeshift bottom inside the box, then returned the other contents. After putting the box back into the chest and covering it over with the clothing and blankets, she closed the lid. She added the journal to the other items within the sack she wished to bring with her. When she had the time and the privacy of her chamber at the castle, she would study it more closely.

Knowing the lord's soldiers would not dwell overlong at the stream's edge before growing suspicious and seeking her out, she quickly looked about the cottage, making sure she had everything she wished to take. She stood in the middle of the front room and closed her eyes, saying a quick prayer to the gods to watch over the cottage until she could return. Then she walked out the door and closed it tightly behind her, slinging her sack over her shoulder before she headed up the pathway, away from her past and toward her future.

~*~

"My lord, may I speak freely?" Cederic asked Tristan.

"Of course." Tristan turned briefly to answer him, but then resumed gazing out the window of the solar. Gemma had left at first light to retrieve her belongings at her cottage in the forest. Though it had only been an hour or so, he was still a little uneasy of the venture and watched the gate with slight concern.

"The peasants, being untrue to their agreement, have given a fraction of that which we had settled upon days ago," stated Cederic grimly.

"Have you confronted them?" He tried to concentrate on Cederic's complaint.

"Aye, my lord, I have. I spoke to the reeve yesterday."

Tristan gave his full attention to his bailiff. "Then why is this so, Cederic? What reason has he given you?"

"The peasants, my lord, say they are awaiting the justice they sought in the matter of the girl."

"The two have naught to do with each other."

He knew Gemma had been brought to the castle to be tried for the crime of attempted theft and murder. He had been meaning to speak with her, but with Fury's illness, he'd not had the time to question her. Too, he had been with her over the past two days she'd been at Haddon. He had glimpsed the kind heart she possessed, and he felt certain she had been falsely accused.

"Aye, my lord, I know it. But the peasants say that since they have been denied justice, you, in turn, shall be denied," Cederic said wearily.

"They dare much with their words and actions!"

"Things have been much turned 'round since the great plague, my lord. 'Tis not just here at Haddon, but all over England. Peasants are in upheaval over rents and labor. They feel they should benefit more from the work they do. They say their lords should pay them wages, and they should all be free to own the land they live upon and have the right to work for whomever they choose."

"What nonsense is this? They do not own the land, *I* own the land! I allow them to raise their families and live on it, and even to grow their food there. What I ask in return from them is more than fair."

"Aye, lord. But things have changed. Many peasants died in the plague, and the ones who remain feel they do twice the work. Thus, they feel they are in a position to bargain with the lords and barons."

Tristan was angry. He, too, had been touched by the plague, he and his brothers having lost both their parents and a younger sister to it. He had blamed himself for being in France fighting for King Edward with his brothers and men when the sickness had struck the rest of his family in England. When they had finally returned, they were met with a gruesome sight. London was ravaged by the sickness, and it seemed everywhere they went they met with death and destruction. God surely must have been angry and punished them, they had all believed. He and his brothers and his loyal soldiers had traveled the countryside. Homeless and full of despair, the only families they now had were each other. Finally, he had been summoned by Edward to return to London. The king had dangled the bountiful trophy of Haddon Castle in front of him. A castle to call his own, a place for himself and his men to stabilize the crumbling foundation their lives had become.

Securing the castle from the traitor Madmont had not been difficult. Tristan had been welcomed as the new lord, and all had seemed well. But being the lord of a castle and surrounding village had been new to Tristan. He was not well versed on the machinations of such a large fief. Then the poor weather had devastated the village fields. Wrestling even meager rents from the peasants had become a challenge. Rebellion he had faced before, but it had been with enemies on the field of battle, where he had suppressed it with the end of his sword. Dealing with a village of unruly peasants was another matter entirely. These were *his* people. They had sworn an oath to him. But recently, all they had done was thwart him at every turn.

"I will speak with Gemma as soon as she returns. She will give me her tale of what occurred in the village. Then I will seek out the reeve myself and relay my decision to have her remain at Haddon to serve as our healer. Thus, justice will be served. I sense there to be much animosity t'wards her from the peasants. She will be safe here."

"Let us hope this will appease them, my lord. I would hate to have to wrest the rents from them."

"I am their lord," Tristan said determinedly. "My word is law."

"Aye, lord, pray that it is, to them," Cederic said grimly. He exited the room to leave Tristan alone to watch for Gemma's return.

~*~

Gemma entered the bailey with her escort and immediately headed for the doors of Haddon. She wished to make haste to the privacy of her chamber so she could examine the contents of the journal she'd discovered. After giving the guard a brief nod, he opened the heavy doors to allow her entry. Hurrying past the great hall, she went directly to the stairs. As she made the turn down the corridor to her room, she ran straight into Tristan's huge chest. He quickly grasped her about the shoulders to prevent her from stumbling backward.

"My lord! I am sorry, I did not see you there."

"Nor I you. But 'tis glad I am we have run into each other." Tristan grinned at his pun. "I need to speak with you."

"Now, my lord?" When she noticed the frown on his face, she added quickly, "I wished to put my belongings in my chamber." She saw him note the sack slung over her shoulder, and he reached out for it. Noticing his intent, she backed up. "'Tis unnecessary, my lord, I can manage."

"Very well. When you are finished unpacking, I wish for you to meet me in the solar. At the top of the stairway, go to the right, then follow the corridor down halfway. There is a door on the left-side that gains entrance to the room."

"I will be along shortly, my lord." She felt anxious now,

not just because of the journal she had secreted away in her sack, but by the tone of his command. He gave her a quick nod and strode away. She hurried to her chamber.

After securing her door, she dropped the sack onto her bed and untied the string holding it closed. Dumping the contents out, she carelessly tossed aside her old clothing and grasped the journal. Clutching it tightly in her hands, she scanned the interior of the chamber, looking for a hiding place. She did not know what the journal's contents may hold, but after all that Adele had confided to her, she wished to take no chances of anyone finding it and mayhap discovering her secret. Finally, she settled on putting it in the bottom of the chest. It contained some sheets for the bed and a warm comforter for cooler nights. She tucked the journal beneath the sheets, then quickly folded her clothing to put on top of everything. Satisfied it was well hidden, she closed the lid of the chest and exited her chamber in search of the solar, and Lord Tristan.

She located the room and rapped lightly upon the door. When she heard him bid her enter, she eased the door open and stepped within. After pulling the door closed, she slowly turned around to face him. He was standing in front of the hearth, which had a warm fire crackling within. His expression was unreadable as he motioned her to come forward.

She cautiously approached him. "You wished to speak with me, my lord?" He was watching her intently, as though contemplating something.

"Aye, Gemma." He took a few steps closer to her and lightly grasped her elbow to guide her over to a chair placed by the hearth. He did not take the other seat across from her but remained standing. "I would speak of the night you came to be here."

She glanced into the flames of the fire. She did not know what he knew of that night. He had yet to question her on what had happened in the village with Daniel. It was more than likely his brothers, and the bailiff had told him they had come upon her and Daniel struggling on the road. They had also likely told him of the accusations made against her. But she also hoped her side of the tale had been relayed. That Daniel had tried to force himself upon her, and she had merely tried to protect herself.

Tristan stood patiently observing her as she mentally went over the story she wished to tell. When she made no attempt to speak, he finally said, "Why were you and the man from the village struggling on the road when my men came upon you?"

She took a deep breath before she answered. "He — Daniel, that is — gave chase after I had run from him at his cottage, my lord," she answered quietly.

"Why was he chasing you?" His gaze was direct as he stared into her eyes.

She dropped her head and looked at the floor, ashamed. "He was angry because I had slashed him with my dagger."

He stepped towards her and reached out to lift her chin so he may again look into her eyes. "Why did you slash him with your dagger?" His tone was curious, not condemning.

"I.... He.... That is.... I was trying to make him release me, my lord." To her embarrassment, tears started to form in her eyes.

"Why was he holding you, Gemma? Was he preventing you from running away after he had caught you attempting to steal from him, as he proclaims?"

"Nay, my lord. I was not stealing from him. He lied. Whilst I was preparing the evening meal, he began to make advances on me. He would have done rape, if I had not struck out at him and escaped."

Tristan's expression became stormy. He walked over to the window, keeping his back turned as she watched him. He finally turned around to face her. "Why did you then escape my men when they were bringing you to me?"

"I was frightened." She took a deep breath to control her emotions before she continued. "I have known Daniel since we were children. Never could I have expected him to act this way toward me. I trusted him, and he betrayed me. Of all the villagers, he is the only one who has ever treated me with a hint of friendliness. I had hoped when I went to the village seeking employment, being amongst them daily may finally breach the distance between us, but it was not to be so. They were quick to think the worst of me. I believe I feared you would as well, my lord."

"I do not know the reasons they act as they do, Gemma. Nor do I think there is anything I could do to make them behave differently. But know this—you are here now, and you may remain here as long as you like, for I accept you." His voice held such warmth that she felt her eyes again fill with tears. Such kind words she had never before heard from any other than Gran.

Tristan approached her and reached out to touch the golden torc around her neck. "How came you by this? It is most beautiful upon you." He seemed mesmerized by the torc that she had tried to keep concealed beneath her collar.

She backed away and hastily answered him. "It was a gift from my mother before she passed away, my lord. I have it with me always, for it makes me feel closer to her."

"An unusual gift. Was your mother not from the village?"

"Nay, my gran raised me. I knew little of my mother, or of where she came from. I was a child when she passed." She hoped he did not notice the sudden tension in her voice.

"A sad tale. But what of your sire—did you know naught of him as well?"

"I knew very little of my mother, and nothing of my sire. I do not believe my gran knew him, for she never spoke of him."

He still appeared entranced by the torc. Gemma walked over to the window, breaking his contact with the sight of it. She looked towards the forest in the direction of the stones—though she could not see them, she could feel them. So intent was her gaze, she did not notice him come up beside her and follow the line of her vision.

"What do you look at, Gemma? Are you regretting your decision to remain at Haddon?"

"My lord, as much as I do love my home in the woods, I was slowly starving there. It was why I went to work in the village. If not for your offer to remain at Haddon, I do not know what would have become of me."

"You return the favor of my hospitality with the offer of your skill. We are much in need of a healer." He pushed away from the window and began to stride towards the door of the solar. "We are finished here, Gemma. I am satisfied by our conversation that you were indeed unjustly accused," he spoke as he briefly paused by the door, and then he was gone.

She breathed a sigh of relief as she sagged against the stone by the window. He had believed her. He had given her his trust and his acceptance. *What a fine day this turned out to be*, she thought, as she left the solar to return to her chamber.

~*~

Tristan was going to the village to kill Daniel.

First, he would speak with the reeve in regards to the rents paid — or rather, the lack of rents paid — then he would deal with the other problem.

After speaking with Gemma in the solar, he had strode directly to the stables. There he had checked on Fury while a stable lad saddled him another mount. Then he had begun to ride to the village.

He must have appeared formidable as he neared the peasants in the fields. They stared up at him in awe as he approached and asked which of them was the reeve. The peasants were disgruntled, though wary, and a few of the braver ones began to voice their displeasure about their demands of justice not being served.

Tristan was consumed with his purpose, and would not allow himself to become more infuriated by the peasant's ranting. He swung off his mount when an old man stepped forward to claim that he was Alfred, the reeve. Tristan barely recalled the man, having spent so little of his time around the peasants or in the village.

"My bailiff tells me there are again unsettled matters regarding the rents to be paid." He looked down upon the old man, his demeanor cold.

"My lord, have you reached a decision 'bout the girl?" Alfred couldn't mask the hope in his expression.

Tristan's stare was chilling as he glared at the reeve, and then at each peasant around him.

"Aye. I have found her to be innocent of the crimes she had been accused of." He continued, "I have set her at Haddon as the castle healer. If any of you have need of her services, it is there you may seek her out. But know this — none of you shall malign her, nor call her a witch again, or you shall incite my wrath." His voice was deceptively calm as he looked at them, daring any to defy his judgment. "I shall have my bailiff, along with some of my soldiers, return on the morrow. I expect the agreed upon amount of the rents to be paid in full. Now, which one of you is Daniel?"

"He not be here, my lord," a man said, stepping forward. "He left the fields to return to his cottage."

"Then kindly point me in the direction of his cottage. I wish to relay my verdict in person." Tristan swung up onto the saddle of his mount.

"'Tis down the roadway, my lord, the last cottage before the edge of the forest." The peasant pointed a finger in the direction he spoke of. Tristan only spared him a brief nod of thanks as he turned and rode off.

After Tristan tied the horse to a post out front, he marched up the pathway and did not bother to announce his arrival before he kicked open the door. Daniel was just entering the front room from the bedroom when he started abruptly at the sight before him. Tristan did not wait for him to realize he was in mortal danger before he stalked forward and grabbed him roughly by the front of his shirt, and threw him across the room.

Daniel landed hard, but swiftly regained his feet, bracing

himself for the onslaught of his lord's fury. He backed away as Tristan advanced with a feral look upon his face. Daniel's back came in contact with the wall, and when he realized he could retreat no farther, he raised up his hands in supplication.

"My lord, why do you do this to me? Pray, what have I done?"

"How does it feel to be the quarry?" Tristan fairly growled his reply.

"My lord, I know not what you mean." Confusion masked his face.

"Do you know that it is a crime to lie to your lord?"

"Pray, what have I lied about, my lord?"

"You lied to my men, and therefore to me, about what happened with Gemma," Tristan shouted, his face bare inches away from Daniel's.

Daniel was taken aback. "This is about the false tales of a girl, my lord? And a witch at that? 'Tis clear she has you under her spell, as she had me."

Tristan grabbed him by the throat and nearly lifted him off the floor as he replied, "That girl now happens to belong to me. And I will have none in this village smite nor slander her ever again. Do I make myself clear?"

"Aye, my lord, very clear," Daniel managed to gasp out before Tristan finally dropped him to the ground. Then, with a terrifying look at Daniel's crumpled form, he strode from the cottage and slammed the door shut behind him.

CHAPTER 6

Gemma sent Hazel to the kitchen for a tray for the midday meal. She wished to remain above-stairs in her chamber to study the journal in private. Sitting before the hearth with the flames warding off the slight chill, she placed the journal in her lap, almost afraid to open it and discover what secrets lay within.

This is foolishness, she thought, for what matters could Gran have possibly written that she did not already know of? Flipping open the worn leather cover, she began to read, suddenly grateful for all the lessons she'd received on practicing her letters over the many years they had been together. It was thought of as unnatural and a waste of time for a woman to learn to read and write, especially when she was naught but a peasant, Gran had explained to her. But she too had stressed the importance of the learning, for one never knew when it would become an invaluable asset.

The words on the first few pages did not make much sense to Gemma until she realized she was reading something that a young girl may write of. It contained mostly an accounting of daily chores and activities for someone of an elevated status. The writer had listed matters such as embroidery and the importance of making neat and careful stitches when sewing tapestry and clothing. It also had notes of the conduct expected when entertaining noble guests, and how to instruct the servants in certain duties. It listed several different dishes to be prepared and the order in which they should be served, and many other obligations in the running of a large household. The lists went on and on, page after page, endless responsibilities and social graces that any young girl of consequence would be required to learn in a prominent household.

Gemma was becoming frustrated with the on-going pages of decorum and was about to give up finding anything remotely telling when she skipped through the pages to the middle of the journal. It was then that the tone suddenly changed from a young girl's duties to a young woman's dreams and desires. The woman wrote of being at a May Day Festival her parents had held at their estate. She'd noted the wonderful and exciting entertainment and the guests she had become acquainted with. But none quite as dazzling as the young man who had captured her fancy, a young knight by the name of Tarquin Alexander....

Dear goddess! This journal was not Gran's but belonged to the Lady Talitha, the woman who may be her mother.

She was stunned and shocked by this discovery, and also very curious. How had Gran acquired possession of this journal? But then, it must be how she'd known of Gemma's mother, and of the origin of the torc. Gran had told her that her mother had practiced the old religion and held ancient beliefs. She must have somehow obtained the journal and learned of Talitha by reading it.

No matter how Gran had come to acquire the journal, Gemma knew she must have believed that Gemma was Lady Talitha's daughter. Gemma could no longer question the truth of her origins. Too many facts remained to brush them off as coincidence. Having been found at standing stones as a child. Bearing a striking resemblance to Lady Talitha—at least according to Adele. Her wariness of Hadden Castle—no doubt due to terrible memories buried deep in her mind. Gemma took a deep breath and closed her eyes, feeling a wave of sadness encompass her over the mother she had lost. Talitha had spent her final moments ensuring Gemma's safety. The final act of a mother's love.

Shaking off her melancholia, she turned her thoughts to the mystery of the journal. Perhaps Adele had left it by her side when she had laid her at the standing stones in the hope she'd survive and know of her mother by someday reading the journal. But Adele had not mentioned the journal when she had relayed her tale. Gemma decided to question her about it when she next saw her.

She continued to read.

A later date in the journal told of a clandestine ceremony held on the first day of August that Talitha's parents celebrated with only a select few guests much later in the evening. The group had entered the forest and lit a large bonfire as a place to gather for a long-ago ritual that was still secretly practiced by descendants of the ancient Celts. Talitha had stood with her mother, who was the high priestess of the ceremony. It had been a special night, for Talitha had finally reached the age of ten and six when she could officially be sanctified into the group as a priestess.

Talitha described in vivid detail the ceremony in which her mother, the Lady Cecila, had passed on the golden torc to her. There had been dancing, and offerings of beautiful bouquets of wildflowers thrown into the fire for the gods, followed by a passing of a jeweled chalice that held a dark red wine that each had drank deeply from. They had honored the god Lugh at this fourth and final festival of the Celtic year, and offered prayers for plentiful harvests and prosperity for the land. They had also asked him to guide, watch over, and protect the priestess, for it was thought that she who wore the torc had the divine attention of the gods.

The knight, Tarquin, had been invited to participate in the ritual, to the delight of Talitha. She had noticed him watching her throughout the ceremony. She had seen him many times throughout the past few months since the first time she had met him at her parents' May Day celebration in the spring. This was the first time he had witnessed and participated in a Celtic ceremony. Inviting him to participate was a show of trust bestowed upon him by her parents. The ceremonies had always been attended by only a chosen few, for many would fear or scorn such old beliefs.

The relaying of the tale by Lady Talitha entranced Gemma. As she turned each page, she became more enraptured in the excitement Talitha wrote about of her feelings of love for the knight, Tarquin. It was obvious the pair was mad for each other, and soon it became apparent to all when Tarquin asked permission of Talith's sire to wed her.

Gemma could almost picture the two of them in her mind, so in love and so happy and excited about the future awaiting them. Talitha wrote of how she and Tarquin shared the same beliefs in the power of the gods and goddesses the Celts worshipped. They shared a mutual love of nature and beauty and ceremonies of olden days almost forgotten in this time. Talitha wrote of her excitement of the anticipated journey to Tarquin's family home in England. She had never been very far from her own home in Wales, and she was consumed by plans she and her family were making to send her off to join with her betrothed. A wedding ceremony would be held at Tarquin's family home, and Talitha was to join him there. She would travel to England with a small train of servants and men-at-arms to escort her to him. Her only disappointment was that her own mother and father would not be accompanying her on her trip. They would come later to attend the joining ceremony, for it was too difficult for them to leave their estate at harvest time.

Talitha's last entry was written on the day she was to leave on her journey. She was happy to be traveling to marry her love, but also sad for leaving her family and beloved home. She wrote of her hopes and dreams of the future she would share with Tarquin. But alas, Gemma knew how the tale would end. Adele had told her of Madmont's capture of Talitha and the brutal slaughter of her train.

She was about to close the journal, thinking it was the end of the story, but by chance, she happened to flip through a few pages following the last entry and noticed there was more of the story to be told.

The handwriting was definitely not Talitha's but possessed the same graceful chirography. The tale began as such.

I received word many days past from Talitha's betrothed that she had not arrived as scheduled. Needless to say, Lord Tarquin is mad with grief and worry over the fate of his beloved. Henry, my lord husband, many soldiers, and I rode throughout the land for many days and nights in search of the retinue. Somewhere along their journey, they had met with misfortune, for we have found scattered effects by the border belonging to my daughter and those in the train who had accompanied her. Amongst the items, much to my dismay, was this, my beloved daughter's journal. We searched out the area, and sadly we have found some hastily covered bodies within the forest belonging to some of the members of Talith's train. There are signs of a struggle, but nowhere, thank the gods, have we found anything to cause us to believe Talitha has been killed. It would appear she has been taken, but by whom we know not. We will continue to search for my daughter and the others. We will not rest until we have discovered what foul deeds hast befallen them.

The entry went on, and Gemma scanned through quickly to the end, where it was signed, "Lady Cecila." This caused her to feel even more confusion, for if Lady Cecila had found the journal, Talitha could not have been in possession of it. Therefore, Adele could not have left the journal at the standing stones to be found alongside the child. That must be why Adele had not mentioned the journal — she had not known of its existence. It left the question as to how Gran could have attained it.

The hour was growing late, the light growing dim in the chamber where she had sat entranced by the story in the journal. A new tale was beginning by Lady Talitha's mother, but Gemma closed the journal and hid it away in the chest. She stood quietly at her window, watching the sun go down, and contemplated the fate of Talitha. What of Cecila and

Henry, Talitha's parents? Where had their search led them? Did they ever learn the fate of their beloved daughter? Most important of all was Lord Tarquin. He could be her sire. Talitha had written of the love they had shared, but she had not mentioned they had, in fact, joined together in intimacy. Gemma had so many unanswered questions, but time was not on her side. She could not remain in her chamber overlong, or Lord Tristan and the others might grow curious as to her whereabouts.

Realizing it was time for the evening meal, she headed to the great hall. The meal was just being served, and she quickly seated herself at the table closest to the door. She wished to remain far from the dais so she may dwell privately on her thoughts. She had no wish for the distraction Lord Tristan's presence would surely present.

She shared a trencher with a pretty young woman who seemed kind and intelligent, but also anxious to catch the eye of every young man who happened to look her way. Gemma noticed her blushing and casting coy glances and smiles at several men seated at the table across from them.

"I think some of those fellows would like to become better acquainted with you, miss," the young woman whispered to her.

"I have no wish to become better acquainted with the likes of those fellows."

The woman grinned at her. "I am Alison. I saw you seated with our lord last eve. Are you the healer who tended his horse?"

"Aye, I am. My name is Gemma. Lord Tristan has asked me to remain here as the castle healer."

"My, your skill must be considerable, indeed, to have tended the lord's own horse."

"I only wish to serve those who are in need of my aid."

"Well, 'tis glad I am for your company. There are few young women 'round this place." Alison boldly returned a wink to a young man walking past.

Gemma noticed the flirting and frowned at her. "You should not encourage him thus. He may get improper ideas into his head about you."

Alison shrugged her shoulders and quickly responded, "Aye, but 'tis such fun to tease."

Gemma could not help but laugh at her new friend's playful manner. They enjoyed the remainder of their meal with easy conversation. Alison told her that she had been at Haddon since the spring. She had come to work as a laundress and was grateful to have found employment at such a large and fine castle. They parted company with promises to seek each other out on the morrow.

Gemma left the castle to go to the stables. She wished to check on Fury to see if he may be in need of another dose of her tonic. As she entered the yard and began walking in the direction of the stables, she noted that although the evening was dark, the moon was bright and cast a glow over the area. She found her way across the yard with no trouble, and was soon inside and approaching Fury's stall. She was not surprised to see Nathan hovering over the animal. He was rubbing a gentle hand down the side of the horse's neck. He turned as she approached.

"Good eve, Gemma."

"And to you, Nathan. How does our lord's horse fare?"

she asked, though she could see for herself that Fury seemed quite well.

"Very well, my dear. Ye have done a fine job of tendin' the animal."

"I had much help, Nathan. 'Tis thanks to you and Lord Tristan's efforts that my tonics were successful."

"Such modesty. Gemma, ye should allow yourself more credit."

She stroked her hand down Fury's sleek neck as she gave Nathan a slight shake of her head to hide her embarrassment over his praise. Feeling satisfied the fever was indeed gone, she turned to bid Nathan good eve.

"Good eve, my dear," he replied as she left the stables.

The day had been long and full of many surprises. Gemma felt the need to sleep, and hopefully, put aside her fears and anxiety about what she had learned and what she would do with that knowledge. She walked slowly across the yard towards the castle, her gait slow and wistful. There was much to occupy her mind, and now that the danger had passed over the lord's horse, she found her thoughts wandering over other matters.

The shock of discovering Gran had possessed the journal of Lady Talitha was again fresh upon her, and it still puzzled her greatly as to how the journal had found its way to the little cottage hidden deep within the woods. Might it be possible that Cecila's search had led her to Haddon Castle? Had she found the daughter she had sought?

Gemma's deep thoughts kept her so engrossed that when she found herself near the entrance to the castle, she decided to remain outdoors and walk slightly further as she pondered the story of Cecila and the mysterious journal. She ventured around to the side of the castle and walked beside the long length of the thick stone wall that loomed high overhead, casting dark shadows over the surrounding grounds. Gemma thought herself to be alone with just her thoughts for company when she broke from her rumination to the sound of footsteps approaching her. She turned around to seek out who had come so quickly and quietly upon her when the clouds blocking the moon suddenly moved aside, and it shone its light upon the face of Lord Tristan.

Gemma released a breath she had not realized she'd been holding. The sight of Lord Tristan's large form dominated the darkness, and as he approached her, she could feel her heart begin to beat rapidly. He made an imposing sight with his broad shoulders and his great height. The closer he moved towards her, the more she felt the need to tilt her head upward to keep sight of his penetrating gaze. The man might have appeared menacing, coming upon her the way he did, finding her alone in the darkness, but she feared him not. Lord Tristan wore a friendly smile upon his handsome face, and she again recalled the heartfelt talk they'd had earlier in the day. He had not censured her words, nor had he found her tale to be false. Instead, he had offered her comfort in her time of distress, and too, he had offered her his acceptance.

Gemma returned his smile, and in spite of the bond they had forged earlier, she felt herself suddenly shy in his presence. She knew not why, but he made her feel things deep within her, things she had not thought existed before now. Things like she was special to him, and it confused her that she wanted it to be true. He was her lord, and she was naught but a peasant. It was not right for her to have feelings for him this way. She lowered her gaze, suddenly feeling shame over her longings for what could not be.

"What is this I see before me?" he asked, causing her to lift her gaze to him. "A beautiful young woman out wandering the grounds at night, with naught but the moon and the stars as her escort?"

She smiled. "I had much to occupy my mind this night, my lord, and I felt the need to be out in the fresh air instead of in my room with my thoughts."

"Have you been to the stables?" If he wondered what preoccupied her mind, he kept silent with his musings.

"Aye, I have, and it would seem your Fury is indeed a formidable animal. There is barely a trace of the sickness that had plagued him earlier."

"I, too, have come from seeing him, and I believe you are correct with your findings. He seems hale to me, and I would give you my thanks for healing him." His appreciation for her skill sounded in his words.

"It was naught, my lord."

"Such modesty is most becoming upon you."

His tone was playful—he must have noticed her sudden discomfort and wished to put her at ease. He made a show of offering her his arm. "May I escort you back to the castle, my lady? Or do you wish to remain alone to ponder your thoughts?"

She smiled, charmed by his courtesy. "I think I shall return with you, my lord. I find the night air is causing me to feel quite sleepy." She tucked her hand into the crook of his arm, the contact sending a sudden jolt of heat between them.

The pair strolled back towards the castle entrance, both silent. As close as their bodies may be, Gemma's mind privately reminded her of the great invisible distance separating them.

Shortly after, when she entered her chamber, she was pleased to see that Hazel had built up the fire. Lord Tristan had left her side at the top of the stairway, telling her he wished to survey the lands from the battlements, as was his nightly habit.

The flames from the fire gave off sufficient light, so she did not need to use a candle to see while she washed and changed from her gown into a clean shift for sleeping. As she opened the trunk to retrieve a shift and place her folded gown within, she was tempted to reach beneath the sheets to find the journal. As compelling as it was to read further into the story of Cecila, she did not give in to the temptation due to the late hour. On the morrow, she wished to rise early and begin setting up the room given to her for use as the castle healer. She needed to see what plants she could find from the forest before it became too late in the year to find fresh growth. The days were growing shorter as autumn was just days away, and the nights were becoming so cool, she feared frost would soon cover the ground and render most plants quite ineffective for her purposes.

She crawled beneath the blankets on her bed and was soon off to sleep, content until the dreams claimed her....

She was running, very fast, through the forest as a mob of angry peasants gave chase. Their torches burned bright and gave off a reddish glow through the trees. She could hear them crashing through the woods, stomping hard upon the forest floor in their pursuit.

"*Kill the witch!*" *they screamed.* "*Burn her.*"

Harder and faster she ran, but no matter which way she turned, the mob remained just steps behind her. She tried to call out, but her voice was snatched up into the wind and carried far away. There was a break in the trees, and she ran towards the clearing, leaping recklessly over a fallen log that crossed her path. Breaking free of the confining forest, she flew across an open field and ran faster and faster. Then, seeming to break away from the very ground before her, a colossal chasm suddenly appeared, obstructing her flight. She stopped and turned, hoping to quickly sprint off in another direction, but alas, her way was blocked by the approach of the angry peasants. They gathered around her and slowly began to move forward, enclosing her within their midst.

He would come. He would save her.

He must, she assured herself over and over, even as her demise seemed imminent. Her warrior would charge forth into the savage group, and he would protect her. She waited, watching the peasants crowd closer as she inched back near the edge of the precipice, while their threats and taunts grew louder and crueler, and still, he did not come.

Falling to the ground, the voices overwhelmed her. She could not breathe, for their proximity almost cut off the air around her. As darkness claimed her and she began to feel herself falling, she wondered why he had not come, why he had forsaken her.

Gemma awoke with a start, aware she was not in her bed, but on the floor beside it. The fire had almost burned itself out while she had endured the seemingly endless nightmare. Strangely, she felt bereft, as though she had been denied requital, waiting for the warrior to rescue her and to castigate the peasants, but he had not come.

Climbing back into bed, she wrapped the blankets about her protectively. She did not need him, she told herself as sleep began to claim her. A valuable lesson had been learned this night — she had only herself to depend upon.

CHAPTER 7

The next morning, Tristan descended the stairs and approached the great hall, hearing sounds of laughter. He took his seat at the dais and held out his cup to a passing servant who held a pitcher of ale. Giles was seated beside him, but Denton had not yet entered the hall.

Tristan scanned the room, but it was not his brother he was searching for. Finally, he spotted Gemma, seated on a bench far across the room. She was talking with Alison, and he could see the laughter the two shared as they waited to break their fast. It was good, he thought, that she had made a friend in the castle. It would make her days more pleasant if she could find acceptance and companionship amongst the castle folk.

As he ate some of the bread and cheese set before him, he watched her, hoping to catch her eye. He spoke of the past day's events with his brother and the men around him, then turned to look at her again. She was looking at him. She smiled, but quickly turned her face away and continued to talk with the young woman at her side.

Denton joined the group with apologies for his lateness.

Tristan and Giles could tell from the satisfied but tired look upon his face that he had found some pleasure late into the night. Before the meal ended, Tristan spied Gemma slipping from the bench with a few words to her friend before she quietly took her leave of the hall. *What task has her so anxious to begin that she would leave so suddenly?* he wondered. He found he did not have much of an appetite this morning, and now his curiosity was piqued. Bidding his brothers and the others around the table a good morn, he left the hall.

He found her behind the castle on her knees in the middle of an overgrown garden that, in better days, had probably supplied much of the vegetables and herbs used. After approaching her quietly, he was standing almost behind her when she heard his footsteps and turned her head upward to look at him.

"My lord, please, you are standing on some garlic."

He looked down at his feet before stepping over to his left. "Is this better?" he asked, his eyes squinting from the sun in his face, a slight smile on his lips.

"Ah, now you are standing on some cabbage, but 'tis all right. I do not think it was edible any longer."

"Tell me, what fascinates you so about this garden that you rushed off in such a hurry?"

"I wished to see the yield of the castle garden before I set off to search the woods for supplies, my lord. I was hoping that here I might be able to find most of what I need."

"And what have you found?" Tristan gestured around the shabby, unkempt area.

"Well, it is a mess, lord. Though I am sure with some effort to clear away the weeds, it may be salvageable for next year."

"Be that as it may, I would have you only leave the grounds with a couple of my men in attendance."

She stood and brushed the dirt from her gown while looking up at him. "Am I to be guarded then, my lord? For I assure you, if I change my decision about being the castle healer, you shall be the first to know it."

"The men are for your own protection, Gemma. 'Tis true, there are some who may dearly love to catch you alone in the forest," he said with a slight smile, though his warning was clear.

She nodded her head toward him, magnanimously. "Then I thank you for your concern, my lord."

"I protect that which is mine, Gemma."

"I will, of course, tell you of my plans before I decide anything, my lord," she assented.

He smiled, pleased with her quick compliance to his wishes. "Then I shall leave you to your task." He gave her a nod before he walked away.

~*~

Gemma watched as Tristan carefully picked his way back through the garden, mindful of the plants she wished to salvage. She found his concern for her safety a comfort, although she was not altogether pleased with the idea of his men following her about every time she wished to go beyond the walls. A sudden memory of the night he had pursued her through the woods so relentlessly flashed in her mind. Surely he only meant that all the people within the castle were under his protection, and he considered her, like them, his responsibility. She went back to sorting through the garden, assuring herself that over time his restrictions would ease.

Later that day, she worked in the small room set aside for her. The table was laden with many herbs and plants laid out closely to the heat of the flames from the large fire. She tossed a few more logs into the hearth, making the little workroom uncomfortably hot. After inspecting the plants, she pushed a few slightly closer toward the heat, hoping to diminish the time it would take for them to naturally dry out. Time was of the essence — there were no prepared herbs in which to tend the ill should the need arise.

The door cracked open suddenly, and an old face peered within. "My lady," Adele whispered, looking around the room before hurrying in and swiftly closing the door behind her. She leaned against it tiredly, her bosom heaving while she tried to catch her breath.

Gemma stepped forward to help the old woman into one of the chairs by the table. "Adele, what is wrong?" She hurried to pour her a cup of ale.

Adele drank deeply before offering her reply. "My lady, I was helping a lass hang some laundry out to dry in the breeze when I saw ye leaving the gardens to enter the castle. I could not follow you directly, but after our task was done, I came to seek you out. Ye must beware, for I have heard some of the servant's whispering about ye."

"What do they say, Adele?" she asked fearfully, taking the seat beside her.

Adele placed her cup upon the table and leaned forward to grasp Gemma's hands tightly in her own. "Some of them, those who have been here for many years, are saying ye resemble our late mistress, Lady Talitha. They have not noticed the torc — 'tis hidden well beneath the gowns ye wear. But if they do happen to see it, my lady...." Her words trailed off, not lending voice to her fears.

Gemma shivered despite the heat of the room. She could well imagine the wrath of Lord Tristan if he were to gain word that she may be Madmont's issue. He may suspect her of treachery, considering how ill thought of Madmont was by him and his soldiers, and especially King Edward. She rose and began to rotate the herbs, the simple task somewhat calming to her fragile nerves.

Adele looked at her determinedly. "My lady, ye must leave this place. I know ye have a place of yer own in the forest — surely ye would be safer there."

"Nay, Adele. Those servants only speculate about my relationship to Lady Talitha, they do not know for certain. Perhaps by remaining here, I may uncover the truth of who might truly be my sire. Too, it was a dire situation I faced before coming to Haddon. I was slowing starving at my cottage in the woods." She sighed as she contemplated her circumstance.

Adele rose. "Please, my lady, tell Lord Tristan ye have changed your mind. Surely he would allow ye to leave, and being the kind man he is, will see that ye have supplies through the winter months."

"If he is so kind, why are you afraid for me, Adele?"

"He is kind to those who mean him no harm, my lady. He suspects naught of ye — yet. If he learns the truth.... Well, 'tis said he is ruthless to those that oppose him, or the king."

"But I do not oppose him. I am no threat to him, or to Haddon."

"Aye, though if he discovers that ye are Lady Talitha's daughter, he will believe ye to be Madmont's issue. Madmont was a traitor to the king. Lord Tristan was sent to expel or to slay all those who be in league with the traitor. Madmont barely escaped with his life before Lord Tristan overtook the walls. If my lord thinks ye to be Madmont's child, he will surely turn ye over to the king to be imprisoned, or worse." Adele shuddered.

Gemma felt sick. She was damned, it would seem, no matter what she decided to do. It was true that entire families could be imprisoned, if only for the fact they were kin to the traitor. Perhaps she could find her true sire, Lord Tarquin? Surely Madmont could not have been her father, for if he were, he would have had no reason to despise her so, or her mother. He must have felt betrayed because the woman he had stolen had not been a virgin. And to make matters worse, she later gave birth to her lover's child. The truth must have enraged Madmont into committing the vile beatings upon mother and daughter.

"I must find proof I am not Madmont's daughter, that in truth, I am the daughter of my mother's betrothed, Lord Tarquin," Gemma said resolutely.

"How, my lady? There be no proof, only speculation. The facts that will concern Lord Tristan will be that Lady Talitha was married to Madmont, and a daughter was born. The daughter did disappear, but now she has returned. He will think ye come seeking vengeance. He will think ye wish to lay claim to that of which belonged to your sire."

"The journal," Gemma gasped.

"What journal do ye speak of, my lady?"

"When I returned to my cottage to gather my things, I discovered a journal hidden amongst my gran's belongings. The journal belonged to Lady Talitha. She had written within all that took place—her betrothal to Lord Tarquin and her plans to travel from Wales to England to wed with him. Then her mother, Lady Cecila, took up the tale and wrote how she recovered the journal from amongst her daughter's scattered belongings. She told of her search for Talitha, and how she strongly feared someone must have taken her. There is more to the story, but the hour grew late, and I feared I would be missed if I did not come down for the evening meal."

"Then mayhap the rest of the story may tell what ye need to discover about Lord Tarquin," Adele exclaimed excitedly.

"I wish there was a way to question the other servants about Lady Talitha without arousing their suspicions."

"There is not much they could tell ye 'bout her. It was I who saw to her needs. She did not go about the castle too freely, being in such fear of the old lord. Though tell me, my lady, how came the old woman who found ye by a journal that belonged to Lady Talitha?"

"That, I am afraid, is as much a mystery to me as 'tis to you."

"Please, my lady, heed my warning. Take the journal and leave this place before it be too late."

Adele anxiously strode to the door to return to her work. She peered quickly around before stepping outside the room and closing the door behind her.

~*~

It was midday, and Gemma sat in her chamber before a cozy fire she had lit in the hearth. While she waited for her plants to dry, she had decided she could spend a little time above-stairs in privacy. She nibbled on some cheese as she read the journal in her lap, enraptured by the tale Lady Cecila had penned so many years ago.

Many more long and cold nights, we have spent scouring the lands for signs of Talitha. As of yet, we have found naught, and the thought of returning home unsuccessful makes our hearts sorrowful. I pray daily to the gods to grant us a sign. I have found a measure of solace in the knowledge that our gods and goddesses will protect the wearer of the torc — our chosen one. In our travels, we came across a band of English soldiers sent from Lord Tarquin of Summit Crag Castle. They, too, were looking for Talitha, but have found no sign of her. I fear we must return home, and soon, for winter will soon be upon us. As much as it pains us to think of ending our search, we know of nowhere else to look.

The journal stopped at that point, but Gemma turned the next few blank pages to where the story took up again.

Returning home to Hally Vale is a sad affair. The mood is somber, for many of the people here and at the nearby farms knew and loved our Talitha. We were relieved to see that our estate is not as ill prepared for winter as we had feared, for many have joined in and helped our workers with their tasks. Tonight I will go into the forest and seek the guidance of the gods. They may give me some sign as to where to search again. Though I fear that as Samhain approaches, the roads will soon become impassable and the weather unbearable for travel.

Here again, the journal ended — for many pages, nothing was written at all. Then finally, toward the end of the last few pages, Cecila again returned to her story.

'Tis with great sorrow I write this entry, for months have passed

since I have last written, and much has happened. I did go forth into the forest on the night I had written last. I lit a fire and pleaded with the gods to grant me a sign of my beloved daughter's whereabouts. So overcome with joy was I when, at last, I did receive that which I sought. From the very flames appeared to me a great figure of a man, and I knew at once he must be our powerful god Dagha. He is the god of life and death and is very skilled at magic. 'Tis well known that Dagha holds great knowledge, for he possesses all wisdom. He did not speak, but instead, a place appeared to me inside the fiery flames; great stones, a colossal formation of them standing upon a slight hill. It was here, at this place, I knew I would find Talitha. So fortunate and excited, I did feel as I raced back 'tward Hally Vale to share my vision with my husband and the others.

My happiness soon turned to horror as I came upon a terrible scene. My beautiful home was engulfed in flames. I could hear the frantic screams of those trapped within, as they desperately sought to escape from the very windows that would lead them to fall to their deaths. I could not enter my home; the closer I got, the more intense the heat became. I could only watch helplessly as my beautiful Hally Vale, with my beloved Henry within, expired before my very eyes.

The horror of that night still haunts me and fills me with such pain. It was all I could do not to lie down and die right alongside my husband and the many others lost. But alongside death, I had also been granted life — the life of my daughter. For I had seen the place where she was taken. The place that I would go.

I gathered from the debris anything of value I could salvage. I found some jewelry and coins, but most miraculous of all was this journal. It was untouched by the devastation, still, in the small, carved chest I had placed it in, safe from the flames of the fire.

I traveled alone and very far through the ravages of nature and the threat of man. I seemed led as if by some unseen hand, guided to the place that I sought. And although I did not yet find my Talitha, I heard from the villagers that their lord, Madmont, had taken a wife a few months past, not long after my Talitha went missing.

I knew I must proceed with caution, for many in the village spoke of their lord as a cruel and ruthless man. I discovered the standing stones, where I again asked for help and guidance from the gods. They answered my plea, for a fox soon appeared, and when I followed, it led me to a cottage nestled deep within the forest and well hidden, I soon discovered, from any other who should seek it out.

Months after my arrival, I heard whispers and rumors that a daughter was born to Madmont and his lady — who I am now all but certain is my beautiful Talitha. It was suspected the child was not his, for she was born too early.

I integrated myself with the villagers as their healer, and though I have remained in this place now for over three years, I have as yet to lay eyes upon my daughter. Every night, no matter the season or the weather, I return to the stones, hoping for a sign that she is well.

I fear for my daughter, and my granddaughter, whom I suspect is truly the daughter of Lord Tarquin. I shall continue to wait and to watch for any signs of Talitha. Though I am not with her, I can sense her presence. And too, I know that she senses mine.

Last eve, I was again at the standing stones and was shocked when a vision appeared to me in the flames. The vision was that of a beautiful young woman standing nigh the Castle of Haddon. She greatly resembled my Talitha, yet she was slightly different. She stood proud and beautiful, dressed in splendor, indicating her as the lady of the castle. Surely, I thought, this must be my granddaughter. But if she is meant to one day be the Lady of Haddon, then mayhap *she is truly Madmont's daughter? I was confused but did not have long to ponder my thoughts, for I heard a faint cry from behind one of the stones.*

I discovered, to my dismay, a small child beaten nigh to death. I quickly brought the child to my cottage, where I tended her. I was at once shocked and rejoicing when I discovered the torc round her neck, for it was my own granddaughter I had saved. I fear my own Talitha has left this earth but has sent me her little daughter to watch over. I will care for the child and love her as my own. But caution shall rule my heart. I shall not tell the child who she is, or in turn, who I am to her. For surely, as she grows, she would wish to seek out Madmont, who she may suspect is her father. I must protect her from his wrath and keep her safe until she can lay claim to that which is her destiny.

Gemma felt numb. She sat upon the floor and stared into the flames of the fire. The writing in the journal had ended with those last words, written so long ago. And now she knew. Knew that the woman who had found her that night when she had been but a child was her true grandmother. Cecila had found her, and had known by the torc she wore that Talitha was Gemma's mother.

So many questions Gemma had had over the years became clear to her now, but also, new questions surfaced. The reason that Gran had kept her hidden from the soldiers was surely because they might recognize her as Madmont's missing daughter. Too, the villagers had seen the torc around her neck, for she was never without it. The soldiers may recognize it, but the villagers would not. They had never seen Lady Talitha, so they could not know it was hers. But there was always the chance that someone in the village would talk about the torc, and word could travel back to the castle of its existence, assuredly causing a search to ensue. The risk of her being discovered was real, but Gran had written of a vision. A vision that Gemma would one day be the Lady of Haddon. This was the reason she'd remained near to the castle and to the danger. She was awaiting the day when Gemma would finally lay claim to that which she felt was her destiny.

She surmised that Gran also did not have anywhere else to go. Her own home, Hally Vale, had burned to the ground, and her husband was dead. But why did she not seek out Lord Tarquin? Perhaps she feared, after so many years had passed, that he had married another? And Gran could only speculate that Lord Tarquin was Gemma's sire — there was no proof. Not to mention, she was the last link Gran held with her daughter. The thought of giving her up may have been too much for her.

The story also answered her question as to how Gran possessed the journal of Lady Talitha. The initials upon the wooden chest, CH, must stand for Cecila Hally. Cecila's fears were also real. Fear that Gemma, if she knew her true identity, would have gone to seek out answers from the dangerous Madmont. She knew she would have surely done that which Gran feared, no matter how great the peril to herself. She did not feel anger for Cecila's actions or her reasoning — the woman had held her welfare and safety in her hands. She had made her feel loved and cherished. Not knowing that the woman had been her true gran had not lessened the love Gemma felt for her.

Now that she had the answers she craved, what could she do with the knowledge? Cecila had named Lord Tarquin's castle as Summit Crag. Could she bring herself to travel there to seek him out? If she did so, what would she say to the man? *Greetings, my lord, you know naught of me, but I am Lady Talitha's daughter, and you may be my sire.* She paced the confines of her little room, pondering her new dilemma. Something that profoundly disturbed her was Cecila writing about her vision of Gemma being the Lady of Haddon. Cecila had questioned the possibility of Gemma's true sire being Lord Madmont. The idea of that evil man being her father made her shake with fear. Nay, she reassured herself, Adele had told her Talitha had given birth to her child early. And what else, other than the sight of watching your wife's child grow more and more each day to resemble her true father, could have sent Madmont into such a deadly rage?

Gemma put the journal back into its hiding place and left her room to return to her work. Entering the little room by the kitchen, she went about collecting the plants and herbs that had almost dried, placing them into separate bundles to be mixed into salves or brews when needed. She laid the bundles upon the work shelves and swung open the shutter of the one window in the room to let in some cool fresh air.

She leaned out the window and gazed toward the lists, where she could see some of Lord Tristan's soldiers practicing at swordplay. The loud crashes of the swords made her shiver, but she watched, fascinated, for she had never before seen men fight with such skill. The men wore chain mail to protect their bodies, and helmets to protect their heads from overzealous blows. One man stood out on the field, preparing to take on two men at one time. The man towered over his two opponents, and she watched in awe as he quickly and skillfully dispatched the two attackers within mere minutes. His squire rushed over to offer him a canteen, his young face smiling broadly at his lord's prowess. The giant accepted the canteen with one hand and reached up with the other to remove his helm.

Gemma was entranced when she saw the unmistakable blond mane of Lord Tristan. She stared in wonder at his powerful form as he lifted the canteen and drank his fill. She felt her humors rise and heat, rushing out of control just at the mere sight of him. As she gaped at him, he suddenly turned to face her direction, his gaze fastening upon her. Quickly she stepped back from the window, hoping she had been mistaken. His stare could not have bored into her so, not from such a distance. No doubt, she was imagining things from all the stress of the last few hours. In an attempt to alleviate her worries, she threw herself into her work. She swept the floor of the little room, wiped the table and the shelves, and rearranged her new supplies of herbs and healing plants.

Soon it was time for the evening repast. She washed her hands and ran her fingers through her tangled hair, wishing she could spare a few moments to go to her room for a comb. She then left to join the others heading for the great hall, not wanting to draw any unwanted attention her way by arriving late. When she entered the hall, she saw Alison was already seated at a table, so she went to join her.

"Greetings, Alison. I hope your day was not too hard spent?"

"Greetings, Gemma. Nay, my day was spent in the usual way, washing and hanging to dry the endless clothes and sheets of the castle folk." She rolled her eyes for effect.

"Poor dear girl."

"And how did our healer spend her day?"

"I went to the castle gardens this morn and my, what a mess it was. I was lucky to salvage some of the plants and herbs I found growing there. I took them to my healer's room and laid them out to dry. I spent much of my day there, and spent some time in my own chamber above-stairs straightening out my belongings." She enjoyed Alison's friendship but did not wish to entangle her in the mess she had suddenly found her life in.

The meal was served, and Gemma was surprised to discover she had an appetite. Alison barely spared a glance at their trencher as she scanned the room, probably searching about for a handsome knight to rest her gaze upon. She watched her friend bat her eyelashes at a handsome young man seated at the end of their table. Gemma sighed as she sipped her ale, wishing suddenly that her own life could be so carefree. Aye, Alison had her many labors throughout the day to keep her busy, but her life was her own to command. She wistfully envied her friend that freedom.

After the meal ended, Gemma asked Alison if she wished to walk around outside the castle yard for a spell, but she politely declined. Alison's intent was also to take a walk, but as a young knight suddenly appeared at her side, Gemma knew her friend had another companion in mind. Gemma bid the two a good eve and left the hall to take in some fresh air before the nights grew too cold.

She stepped outside the doors of the castle and headed off in the direction of the lists, around the back of Haddon. She strode briskly, wrapping her arms about herself, wishing again she had not been forced to flee the village, leaving her only cloak behind.

The evening was growing dark, the night air cool and crisp. Leaning against the stone wall outside her healer's room, she gazed around, replaying in her mind's eye the exchange between her and Lord Tristan. As she stood there, she honestly examined the feelings that coursed through her when their eyes had met. It felt like pure fire, the heat his look had stirred within her. He had made her feel such longing during those endless moments — but for what, she knew not. She'd felt as though they were the only two people in the land.

She pushed away from the wall and cursed herself for being a romantic fool. What was she but a peasant outcast, trapped and hiding within the lord's realm? Had she meant anything to him, it would be for a meaningless tumble, followed by a curt "by your leave." She must not forget who she was — the daughter of a traitor to the crown, or perhaps the bastard of a man who knew naught of her existence.

She wrapped her arms tightly around her sides as a sudden chill took her. It was not just the cold that made her tremble so, it was also the fear of discovery. Her position was perilous, fraught with risk of exposure, and mayhap, even disaster. Lord Tristan had been kind to her. Indeed, he could have distrusted her tale and delivered any form of punishment. Instead, he had listened to her and comforted her and even offered his friendship and protection.

And how had she repaid his friendship? With deceit and secrecy. Truly, she conceded, it had not been her intent. She had not known the entire tale of her identity and the events which had ensued so many years ago. She had only just learned the story herself. Really, she had not been deceptive. She'd had her suspicions, especially after talking with Adele, but she had not had any real facts to give credence to the tale.

But she now had the facts. The problem presented was she did not know what to do with her findings. If she were to go to Lord Tristan and tell him her tale, what action would he take? Would he be obligated to turn her over to King Edward? Being the daughter of a conquered traitor, she might become his ward, to do with as he pleased, or to dispose of however he wished. Be it to a convent, or as wife to one of his men, or even to rot within his dungeon. Or might he wish to give her the benefit of the doubt and take her word and her reasoning that she was more likely the daughter of Lord Tarquin?

She wished she could know for certain what his decision would be, for her fate, and surely even her life rested in his hands. Should she take her chances within the walls of Haddon for the winter months, and hope none of the older servants recognized her as Talitha's daughter? But suspicion was already being cast her way. Or should she leave? Wait until the morrow when the gates would be open and flee to her cottage, praying to the gods Lord Tristan would not seek her out. Could she sustain herself throughout the winter if she did?

An even more daring and drastic thought was to leave before the roads became impassable by snow and ice and seek out Lord Tarquin. If she could somehow make him believe she was Lady Talitha's daughter, then perchance he would take pity on her and let her stay within his walls for a time. If she were to show him the journal she possessed, he might liken the possibility that he could be her sire. Was it a chance she dare take?

"Now, there is a young woman who is deep in thought."

Gemma started as she heard Lord Tristan's voice come from the darkness behind her. She quickly spun around and discovered he was much closer than she realized.

"My lord!" She attempted to gain control over the sudden riot of emotions arising within her. Gemma was pleased with his presence, but also very much afraid—afraid she would betray the thoughts coursing through her mind. She pasted a bright smile upon her face as she gazed up at him, and prayed her expression did not show the turmoil she felt.

"It is a fine night for a breath of fresh air."

"Aye, my lord." She suddenly felt shy being so near to him. It was not like they had never been alone together before, but now, knowing all the secrets she held, she felt wary of his company.

"Why did you not bring along your cloak when you ventured outside?"

She felt shamed before him. She did not wish to tell him she possessed only one cloak, and that she had left it behind when fleeing from Daniel's attack. But she also had no wish to lie to him, so she offered him the truth.

"I am afraid that in my haste to leave the village, I had to leave my only cloak behind."

Before she could protest, he unhooked the clasp of his own cloak and swung it over her shoulders, wrapping it securely around her. Instead of releasing it, he pulled her toward him and lifted her chin gently. Before she knew what he was about, he lowered his head and gently brushed his warm lips across her mouth.

Tristan's lips were gentle at first. Then Gemma felt his arm reach around behind her back and pull her in tight toward him. His kiss became more intense, more seeking, as she felt his tongue slip lightly over her lips, then seek entry into her mouth. She adjusted to the sweet assault and felt her own tongue join in the teasing dance. Her body warmed and molded toward his solid muscular form. He was so large and hard, strength fairly radiated from within him. She clung to his shoulders, feeling as though she were drowning and growing weak. When finally he released her, she was grateful for the strong arm still wrapped securely around her, or she would have surely sunk to the ground. He released her and stepped back a pace.

"Forgive me, Gemma. I did not mean to behave so."

She quickly reined in her swirling emotions over the encounter. "Nay, there is nothing to forgive, truly." She returned his gaze and smiled, though she felt herself flushing over the sudden tension between them.

He stepped toward her again and reached out to take hold of her hand. "It was not my intention to seduce you when I came looking for you. Though I should say, we would make a fine match, you and I."

"I would know naught of such things, my lord," she said crisply, removing her hand from his. He lifted her chin, which had dipped low, her eyes facing the ground before her. She could see the heat in his determined stare. She backed away from his touch, afraid of him now, for she knew that look all too well.

"Come with me to my room this night. I would be a most sensitive and gentle lover, I vow."

"My lord!" she gasped, backing away farther. "If 'tis bed sport you seek this eve, then I suggest you find someone who would welcome your attentions, for I most assuredly do not."

He frowned. "Then I suggest to you, Gemma, that in the future you do not tempt me again with such a passionate response to my advances. I vow, woman, your charms would tempt a saint." With that, he stomped off into the night, leaving her alone in the darkness.

CHAPTER 8

Gemma returned to her room, shut her door firmly, and leaned against it, wishing there were a bolt upon it she could throw. Glancing around the room, she saw that Hazel had seen to lighting the fire. Gratefully she went before it, feeling chilled. As she reached her hands towards the warming flames, she noted with dismay that she still wore Lord Tristan's cloak. Swiftly, she undid the clasp under her chin and removed the suddenly offensive mantle from her body. Laying it over the chair beneath her window, she returned to the heat, sinking down on the floor before the hearth.

Tears formed in her eyes, and she rubbed her hand across her face angrily, not allowing herself to give in to despair. She felt shocked and ashamed that Lord Tristan would think so callously of her. How could he assume she would willingly bed him after sharing a single kiss? It *had* been a fiery kiss, she admitted to herself. Helplessly, her body had become carried away with a longing she could not identify.

Chastising herself, she made ready for bed and climbed beneath the blankets. Her thoughts began to tumble over themselves, and as she lay alone in the dark, she prayed to the gods that sleep would claim her this night.

~*~

Tristan paced before the hearth in his own room. His mood was foul after his encounter with Gemma, and he had not wished to seek the company of his men in the great hall. How could he have made such a mistake about her intent to join with him this night? After the way she had responded to his kiss, he had thought her to be a more than eager partner for a night's pleasure.

He pounded his heavy fist against the stone mantel with frustration, ignoring the stab of pain. Except for admiring Gemma's skill at healing, he was beginning to regret the day he had ever brought her within the castle walls. Over the past few days, he had thought of little else besides kissing and holding her. Perhaps the villagers were correct when they called her a witch, for he had never felt so enamored of a woman before. Had she bewitched him?

"Damn!"

His thoughts were becoming as crazed as the villagers themselves. Gemma was no witch. Aye, she was a beautiful and desirable woman, but that was all. He had been too long without a woman, for none of the females at Haddon remotely tempted him. And since he had laid eyes on Gemma, even Alison, with her many charms, had failed to lure him to her bed.

He threw off his boots and proceeded to remove the rest of his clothing, all the while deep in thought over what had transpired this eve. Had he been too aggressive, he wondered? But he could find no fault with his deportment. She had welcomed his affection, of that he was sure. Perchance he had been too forward in asking her to accompany him to his bed? She had recently barely escaped being misused by that knave from the village. It could be she was a maid—she was quite young yet.

Aye, he thought, that must be the reason. She was an innocent, and his suggestion had surely upset her. On the morrow, he would offer his apology for his beastly conduct. The poor girl was probably considering running off back to her home in the forest, fearing the safety of her virtue if she remained. And that would never do, for now that he had her in his castle, he would not let her get away so easily.

~*~

Gemma planned to escape the perils of Haddon. Not only was she in danger of discovery of her true identity, but now she had ignited the ire of the lord himself. What had she been thinking to kiss the man like that? After spending a fitful night tossing and turning, she rose before dawn and contemplated fleeing. Before she could think through the consequences of her actions, she stuffed her journal into the bottom of her satchel and covered it with her clothing. Tying the drawstring tightly, she slung the bag over her shoulder. She left her room and forced herself to walk swiftly, but calmly, down the passageway and down the stairs to the kitchen. With any luck, it was too early for the cook to be up and about yet—she hoped to obtain a few supplies before she was on her way.

Luck was indeed on her side, and she breathed a sigh of relief upon finding the kitchen not yet stirring with the morning preparations. As she shoved a couple of loaves of day-old bread, some cheese, and apples into her satchel, she questioned herself again over the haste in which she was leaving. Was the danger really so great? Mayhap she was acting recklessly. What did her cottage in the woods have to offer her besides assured penury? *Safety.*

One thing she was certain of — the risk was far too great to remain here. She resolutely headed towards the doors of Haddon and the posted guard. He swung open the heavy doors, apparently thinking nothing amiss with her making off into the yard before the dawn had even lighted the day. Gemma walked outside and shivered, for the past eve's chill remained in the air. As she headed toward the gate, she had a fleeting regret of not bringing Lord Tristan's cloak along to shield her from the wind. Nay, she would not give the man any excuse to follow her, and perhaps even accuse her of theft. Surely, she thought, the gods would watch over her. With that determined thought, she strode towards the gate. When she was challenged, as she knew she would be, she was ready to offer an excuse for her venture beyond the walls of the castle.

"I require more healing plants for the care of your lord's horse. They must be gathered whilst the dew of the morn is still upon them," she lied, but most convincingly, as soon the portcullis was being raised to allow her exit.

She strode out the gate releasing a great sigh of relief, and as she began to walk down the roadway, she smiled over her success but also worried over what fate would have in store for her now.

~*~

"What do you mean she left before the dawn?" Tristan demanded of the two guards who had ventured forward to the dais to answer to their lord in the matter of the missing healer.

He had entered the great hall after dawn to break his fast, only to be told by Giles the girl had left the gate early this morning. After his initial rage and disbelief had simmered, he learned from his brother that the guards, feeling slightly uneasy of the venture, had come to ask Giles if her tale was true. Giles, knowing Tristan had made clear to him and Denton that if Gemma left the castle walls, she was to be escorted, had instinctively known the girl had fled. Now the two guards stood before their furious lord and stammered out the hasty story she had given them.

"We know the girl was tendin' your horse, my lord. And she did say she had to gather the plants whilst the dew was still upon them. It was the only reason we allowed her to leave the gate," one of the men said.

"And did my orders for her only to leave with escort escape your ears?"

"Well, we did think upon that, my lord. But we figured it being so early and all that an escort would not be necessary. Too, we thought perhaps the girl did not wish to wake any from within the castle to accompany her before first light," the other answered.

"Get to the stables. Both of you. Now! Fetch the girl and right the wrong you have committed!" Tristan shouted.

Both men fled the hall and went immediately to the stables for their mounts.

Tristan leaned back in his chair with an agitated sigh. Giles regarded him thoughtfully and chuckled as he began to dig into the trencher of food before him.

"Does something amuse you, brother?"

Giles looked at Tristan's serious façade and answered, "Aye, it would seem the chit has managed to elude another de Bohon brother. I daresay, Tristan, you are in for a merry chase."

~*~

Gemma glanced around the small tidy cottage she had not thought to see again so soon. Everything appeared the same. It was as if time had stopped when she had left this place, awaiting her return to begin again. A light scratching at the door made all her fears of being found return in full force. The door, which had not been shut tightly, creaked open and revealed a fox, who sauntered within. She smiled in relief.

"Greetings, little friend. Have you come to welcome me home?"

She set her satchel down on the table and reached inside for a loaf of bread. Breaking off a piece, she held out her offering to the little fox, who promptly ran over and snatched it up. Swallowing it in one great gulp, it licked her outstretched fingers. She ran her hand over the fox's sleek reddish coat and broke off another little piece of bread. That, too, was quickly devoured, and when he looked at her for more, she regarded him sternly.

"That will be all for now, little one. We need to make what paltry amount of food I have last."

The first task she began was starting a fire in the hearth to take the chill from the cottage. Lacking in food and clothing, she at least had wood for her fire. When the flames began to dance and give off comforting heat, she emptied her meager supplies on the high shelf in the cooking area, safe from the fox's greedy reach. She picked up her satchel and strode into the bedroom to unpack while the little fox curled himself into a tight ball before the fire. Sighing, she tucked the journal beneath her clothes and extra blankets in her trunk. Her hopes had been high when she left her cottage just days ago, and now she was right back where she had started.

~*~

Afternoon was well upon the men who diligently searched the surrounding forest of Haddon, but not a trace of the missing healer had been found. Tristan had given the men the task, being loath to search for her again. Filled with anger, he feared the violence he might do if he found her himself. But when the morning stretched into afternoon, his temper finally cooled enough to join the pursuit.

He guided a now completely recovered Fury over to a small stream to drink. Weary and frustrated with the continued failure in the endeavor, he dismounted and took his ease to slake his thirst with the cool, refreshing water. He tilted back his head and gazed up at the sky as if to find the answers there. Closing his eyes, he concentrated. He knew she must be near. It was as though he'd followed a trail of her fear and unease, and it led him to this place. He was an expert hunter, a master at searching out and finding his prey. But this somehow seemed different, more urgent, as though he needed to protect Gemma and keep her safe from peril.

It was then he spotted the little red fox on the other side of the stream by the forest's edge. He peered at it, startled by the bold assessing gaze the animal gave him as if it was sizing him up. Fury's ears perked up, and he snorted at the arrival of the little creature.

"Fear not, little friend. I do not seek you out this day. 'Tis another I search for."

The fox strolled forward until it was directly across from Tristan. It gazed at him for a moment before running back to the edge of the forest. When it turned to regard him again, Tristan gave his head a shake, for surely the animal could not be beckoning him to follow? The fox trotted back toward him before dashing off again to the edge of the forest.

Tristan rose slowly, careful not to startle the animal. Grasping Fury's reins, he led him on foot toward the fox. When he got within a few feet of it, it ran off into the forest but stopped every now and again to make sure he still followed. He was beginning to think he was losing his mind when he was eventually led into a clearing. Looking around for the fox, he saw the animal had disappeared, and before him stood a small cottage.

~*~

Gemma sat on her bed, the journal clasped tightly in her hands. Having re-read the entries over and over, she'd hoped she missed some valuable piece of information the first time. Desperate to find something within the pages, she'd searched for some proof of who her true sire was. But there was nothing. Still, she did not know for certain if her sire was Lord Tarquin or the evil Lord Madmont. She sighed and replaced the journal in her trunk, and then ventured into the kitchen to eat a little of the bread and cheese she'd taken from Haddon's kitchen.

As she walked past the hearth, she called out to the little fox. "Time to wake, little one. Join me, and I shall see your belly filled, at least for today." She looked about for her visitor, but he was not before the hearth where she had last seen him.

"Where are you, little fox?"

The door of the cottage suddenly crashed open.

To her horror, Lord Tristan appeared before her, and the look upon his face was one of pure fury. She let out a scream and tore into her bedroom. As she scrambled to climb out the window, strong hands grasped her waist and yanked her roughly inside the room. He spun her around and shoved her upon the bed. He glared at her from his great height, and when she finally freed the hair from her face and peered up at him, she wished that she had not.

"H…how did you find me?" she finally stammered.

His visage had not changed—he still scowled like a formidable warrior ready to do battle. "I thought I had made it clear to you. There is no place you can run that I cannot find you."

"B…but, 'tis impossible. No one has ever found this place. Only Gran and myself knew where it was." Indeed, it was true. Even though she'd led his men to the nearby stream, she had left them behind, not only for privacy but to keep her cottage's location a secret.

"It is but past the stream from over yonder. It was not hard to find."

She gazed wistfully at the doorway to the other room, feeling very frightened and terribly vulnerable, lying in a heap on her bed before this man. "What do you here, my lord?" she ventured innocently. She knew he had searched her out to return her to Haddon.

"I would think that would be obvious." Light glinted from his narrowed eyes.

She climbed off the bed slowly, watchful of him. He made

no move to stop her, and soon she stood in front of him and tilted her head back to keep contact with his eyes. "Am I your prisoner then, my lord? Am I not free to return to my home?"

"Nay, you are not my prisoner. But I thought we had an agreement. You were to remain at Haddon under my protection to act as the castle's healer." He spoke slowly as if he were reasoning with a naughty child.

"And did that bargain include my becoming your whore, my lord?" Her tone was sharp with the sting of the past eve's humiliation.

He grasped her shoulders in his powerful hands. "You seemed willing enough for my kiss last eve. It appeared to me then that you might enjoy a night spent in my bed. But it seems I was mistaken. I had meant to ask your forgiveness, but when I entered the hall this morn to seek you out, it was brought to my attention you had fled the castle. My men and I have been searching for you the better part of the day."

"Oh."

"I would ask you now, Gemma, will you forgive me?" His eyes searched hers. He no longer looked angry, only appearing sincere in his regret.

"I will. As you say, the blame cannot be laid solely upon you. I admit I did enjoy your kiss, but I never thought to take it further than that. I beg your forgiveness as well, for having you think that I would."

He stepped away from her with a brief nod in acceptance of her words. "Peace then, Gemma." He strode to the door of the little room but stopped to cast a look upon her. "I shall wait for you to gather your things, and then we must be off. I would return to Haddon before the moon crests the sky," he said before walking into the front room.

Gemma was not certain how to proceed. Should she capitulate and do as he bid her? Or should she stand fast to her decision to remain at her cottage, safe from the whims and ever-present danger she faced from him, and from Haddon? *Aye*, she thought. *I shall be far at the cottage, far from curious and suspicious eyes.* Resolved, she strode into the front room to confront him.

"My lord?"

"Aye, what is it?" He turned to face her.

"I have decided that I wish to remain here." She held up her hand to forestall the argument sure to come, then continued. "If you or any at Haddon have need of my services, you can send a crier into the forest, and I shall come at once." She spoke quickly before losing her nerve.

His expression once again became stormy. He stalked forward, and as he advanced, Gemma retreated. She looked upon him beseechingly.

"Please, my lord, do not force me to return with you to Haddon."

He halted, momentarily stayed by the fear he must have seen on her face. "Gemma," he began, his calm tone in contrast with his tense stance. "It is not safe for you to remain here. I would have you secure at Haddon, with warmth and substance, to see you through the winter."

She faced him bravely, determined to make him see she was not his to protect, nor to instruct. "I shall be well, my lord. I have lived in these woods for many, many years. I can see myself through the winter, and I need no protection."

He was losing his patience. "Aye, you were so capable of

providing for yourself you nearly got yourself raped in the process."

She was stung by his blatant reminder of that terrible night. "Be that as it may, my lord, I do not wish to return."

"Why in heaven's name not?" Tristan nearly shouted.

She did not know how to respond to his question. Was now the time to tell him all? Should she reveal her fears and secrets? Could she trust in him to hear her tale and not judge and condemn her as a traitor?

As she opened her mouth to begin, a crack of lightning suddenly turned the darkening room aglow. They both ducked their heads in reaction to the vicious assault as the sky let loose its fury upon the land.

"God's blood!" Tristan exclaimed. He strode to the door and wrenched it wide, revealing the chaos of the storm that mounted, already drenching the cottage with heavy rain. He slammed the door shut and turned to her. "It would seem we are not meant to leave here this night," he said grimly.

She looked fearfully at him, wondering what other surprises the night would hold for them both.

CHAPTER 9

The sudden storm did much to add to the discouragement of the small band of men who camped within the forest. Their number was just under two score with their leader included. They had camped as close to the castle of Haddon as they dared. Their self-perceived might far-exceeded rational thought in the risk they faced. Bravery rivaled foolishness, for if they were discovered, it would be their deaths.

These were not men to call to their breast a family to love — they were an evil group. They would slit a throat while smiling falsely into an unsuspecting face of a man, and they were good for naught besides robbing, pillaging, and killing — perfect companions for the man they called their lord. A man more treacherous than the lowest of the company he kept — the ousted Lord of Haddon Castle, Edwin Madmont.

The men sat huddled upon fallen logs pushed around the tiny fire they had built. The flames gave off more thick smoke than warmth as the splash of rain fell upon them. The men grumbled their dismay as they removed from the pit the two plump rabbits they had attempted to cook. The meat was still quite raw, and the men grew even more unruly and angered over the thought of going hungry another night.

Having invaded the forest of Haddon just the eve before, Madmont's plan was to return to the castle when all would think him long gone. He would then reclaim that which had been taken from him when the men within grew lax in their vigilance to guard the keep. And now the time was right, the moment was upon them. Earlier in the afternoon, one of his men had spied Lord de Bohon leaving the gate, and he had not yet returned.

Madmont rubbed his chilled hands in anticipation. Tonight would be the night he would take back his castle at long last. When Lord de Bohon had overtaken Haddon, Madmont had been forced to flee with only a handful of his men. He had found some others in his race for freedom who had also eluded capture or had been turned out when they refused to swear fealty to the conquering lord. Forced to live upon the land like common thieves and beggars, they had preyed upon unsuspecting villages they had camped close to. Madmont had stayed away from Haddon, but he had not gone far. He'd bided his time, and as the months sped by, his thoughts had been filled with revenge.

A plan ran through his mind as he scanned the forest around him. He would divide his group of men into three and place them strategically around Haddon's walls. One group would force open the back gate, which was rarely used or guarded, as it opened up at the edge of a forest that spread out endlessly beyond the castle. The other group would scale the wall at its side, the pounding rain hampering those within to detect the movement upon it. And lastly would be Madmont's group of a dozen or so men. They would lay in wait, just beyond the edge of the forest, for the others to enter. If all went as intended, his men would overtake the guards and raise the portcullis for him to enter.

As he plotted, his men filled their hungered bellies with strong wine. Their minds grew fuddled, and their movements became slower and more exaggerated, their voices becoming louder, gaining the attention of their lord, who had left them too long to their own devices.

"Fools!" he raged. His angered voice caused those seated to surge to their feet. "Make ready, we attack tonight," he hissed at them, his desire for revenge so strong he did not stop to consider the condition of his men. Blood pounded in his veins, and the sudden heat of his body fueled his resolve to take on the task this night. He would be denied no longer.

~*~

The storm progressed, showing no sign of easing before the night's end. Tristan bent low over the fire, adding more fuel to the flames to ward off the chill in the air. He had gone out earlier, when the storm had started, to send Fury off. The rain had not looked to be ending anytime soon, and there was no shelter for the animal at the cottage. Fury, as if understanding his master's command, had galloped off into the forest in the direction of Haddon.

Gemma sat at the table and regarded Tristan's broad back, and again cursed herself for a fool for almost confiding her perilous tale. The tension in the room was tangible, both of them feeling uneasy with the swift change of events.

Tristan was still insistent that she return with him, certain she would perish if left on her own, while she, secure in her resolve to remain at the cottage, had argued endlessly until finally realizing the man was deaf to her pleas. After pacing the room in anger for what seemed like hours, she had finally given in to fatigue and took her ease at the table.

"Please, my lord, can you not see reason in this matter? If you are so worried about my welfare, then perhaps you could supply me with the things I need in exchange for my healing services." She tentatively broached the delicate subject once again.

"You shall have all of the things you need, even the things you merely want, but it will be at Haddon that you have them. I will not have my men searching the woods aimlessly for you every time someone at the castle ails or is hurt. Nay, you shall return with me as I have said." His tone left no room for more discussion.

She sighed and rose from her seat and walked toward the little bedroom. As she reached the door, she turned to him. "I am weary, my lord. I will bid you good eve, I am for bed."

He stood. "I wish us to make an early start for Haddon tomorrow morning."

She gave him a nod and went into the little room, swinging the door shut behind her. She was angry he would not consider her feelings in the matter at all. Instead of making ready for bed as he assumed she would be doing, she was plotting her perilous escape. She knelt before her trunk and opened the lid silently and reached for another of her gowns. Being without a cloak, she would need the extra garment to help shield her from the wind and rain.

After donning the gown, she eased the shutter back from the window she'd secured earlier when the rain began. She wiggled through the opening and dropped down to the soggy ground outside, then dashed off into the nearby woods.

Quickly she ran through the forest as thunder and lightning crashed around her. She ran blindly, without thought to where she was going, so desperate was her flight. Moments after she had scrambled out of her window, her clothing had been drenched through, the extra layers now an added burden. She slowed her pace and began to search the dark woods for any type of shelter, something that would protect her from the rain and wind and hide her from the man she knew without a doubt would be in fast pursuit of her.

She came upon a huge old tree that had been dead for many years. The trunk was still upright and intact, but one side had been burrowed out, perhaps being the home of some forest creature, now thankfully unoccupied. There was just barely enough room for her to crouch down and fit herself into the small opening. It was a snug fit but offered protection from the storm. She twisted about a little, making herself comfortable, resigning herself to the long, fitful night ahead.

Gemma lost all sense of time as the rain continued endlessly, and dampness soaked the ground she crouched upon. She had passed the point of freezing some time ago, and now numbness settled upon her limbs and made her body feel heavy and uncomfortable. Not much later, she finally gave in to her exhaustion and let sleep claim her.

She dreamt of being warm, of sitting before a roaring fire within the circle of the standing stones. The surrounding land was dark until the sudden glow of torches held by an angry mob of villages came upon her.

Their cries for vengeance were aimed at her, and she knew she must flee the warmth of the fire if she were to escape their violent intentions. They chased her through the woods, and she came upon the huge chasm that set her upon the precarious edge of danger. Trapped as they encircled her, she cried desperately for aid but feared the worst, knowing none would come for her. And as the villagers moved in closer and she was forced to the very edge of destruction, it came...a voice from beyond the darkness, reaching out to her like a beacon of light and salvation. The villagers were forced aside as her champion emerged from behind them, sitting atop a huge, formidable destrier. He approached her and held out his hand, and she did not hesitate to take it. He pulled her onto his horse before him and rode off into the night, holding her safely in his powerful arms, leaving the angry mob behind them to the darkness.

Gemma jolted awake with a start. It took her a moment to realize she was no longer ensconced in the tree trunk. She focused on the looming face above her and recognized Tristan, concern etched in his features. He was holding her securely in his arms, and she noticed he had removed his cloak and had her wrapped securely within its folds. She gazed at him in wonder and awe, for he had come for her, truly, just as he had in her dream. Reaching up, she brushed her fingers over the curve of his cheek.

"My lord, do I yet dream, or are you real?" she asked wondrously before slipping back into an exhausted sleep, barely hearing his reply.

"Aye. I am here. You are safe."

~*~

Tristan lifted Gemma's slight form and began the trek back in the direction of her cottage. Miraculously, the rain began to ease off. Still, he questioned the path he'd chosen. But as the small stream near the cottage came into view, he increased his pace with more determination. Before long, he came upon the clearing in which the little cottage sat. As he approached the door and kicked it wide with his foot, he was relieved he'd had no trouble finding the way back.

Directly, he strode into the little bedroom and laid his precious burden upon the bed. Removing his soaking cloak from her, he hesitated only slightly before removing the rest of her clothing. Humorously he chuckled as he began stripping away the second gown she had donned. *What a reckless little fool*, he thought, as he laid her gowns over the trunk to dry. Then he pulled the covers up across her naked form. To check for fever, he brushed his fingers lightly across her brow and, without thought, gave her a chaste kiss upon her forehead before he left the room.

He went directly to the hearth and added more logs to the dying flames. Soon a warm, crackling fire blazed again, and he began removing his own sodden clothes. Laying his breeches and tunic across the back of one of the chairs before the fire, he stood in front of the heat to keep from catching a chill.

Despite the hot flames, the room was still cold. Quietly he stole into the bedroom to look for a blanket to cover himself. He gazed briefly upon Gemma's sleeping form before he removed her gowns from the trunk. He took the gowns into the front room and placed them by the fire. Everything would be dry by morning, he told himself, and he would have no more delays returning to Haddon. Then he returned to the little bedroom to search through the trunk for an extra blanket to wrap himself in.

He lifted the lid of the trunk and began searching the

contents within. Finding what he needed did not prove an easy task — the room was quite dark. He did not wish to light a candle for fear it would disturb Gemma. As he was sifting through the trunk, his hand suddenly encountered something hard near the bottom, buried under what felt like blankets and perhaps some clothing. Curious, he grasped the object and drew it forth. It appeared to be a book of some sort, but he could not be sure, as darkness obscured the cover.

He was about to return to the hearth so he could see it more clearly when he heard a sudden rustling coming from the bed. He glanced towards Gemma, and through the darkness, he could see her sitting up, the blanket clutched fiercely in her grip. She peered at him, and then at the lid of the trunk, which was still swung wide, then she threw back her head and screamed "Nooo...!"

Tristan dropped the book into the trunk and rushed over to the side of the bed in time to gather her in his arms before she screamed again.

"Help me! Please...."

She was trapped again within the clutches of some terrible nightmare, he reasoned, as he held her tighter and spoke in soft, soothing tones, trying to allay her fears. "Hush, my darling, I have you, you are safe."

Gemma, still shaking, frantically clutched at his arms and begged, "Do not leave me, please stay. I am afraid."

She clung to him so pitifully he did not know how to respond. He was still unclothed but did not wish to leave her side, even for the little time it would take to grasp a blanket from the trunk. Reluctantly he slipped beneath the blankets and wrapped his arms securely around her shivering form.

She snuggled painfully close to him and laid her head upon his chest.

He stared up at the rafters of the little room and silently begged the morn to come and put an end to this treacherous night.

~*~

Sometime during the middle of the night, Gemma woke to find herself wrapped tightly in a warm embrace. She lay still for a moment, trying to recall the events before she found herself where she was now. It soon became clear to her she was safe and warm. And unclothed. Lying in bed with her lord. Tristan.

Instead of feeling horrified as she properly should, she instead looked at the man who was now snoring softly at her side. A peaceful, lighthearted feeling stole over her. She brushed a kiss on his broad chest, where her head still rested. When he did not stir, she grew even bolder and began to run her hand softly down his muscled arm. Gemma knew her brazen behavior should shock her, but it did not. She felt gratitude and admiration for this man who had risked the terrible storm to seek her out and return her to safety. Too, she knew he had not taken liberties with her when she had lain unclothed and vulnerable, but instead offered her security and comfort.

Vaguely she recalled awakening earlier to her own screams and seeing him standing across the room. Reaching out to him, she remembered him holding her and calming her with his soft, sweet words. She had begged him to stay with her. Chivalrously, he had slipped beneath the blankets to hold her tightly in his strong embrace. She'd been so afraid, terrified the nightmares would return to haunt her. But they had not, and she had drifted off into sweet oblivion, nestled in his arms.

Gemma was confused over the sudden stirring in her breast. She felt emotions, new and strange to her, in regard to this man. He cared for and desired her, but he was her lord. She could never be anything more to him than his whore. But at this moment, she did not care.

She admitted to herself that she wanted him—even if for only one night, she wished to be his. Her desire must have awakened him, for she felt him begin to stir. His arms tightened firmly around her, and he placed a kiss upon her head. She startled him when she lifted her heated gaze and said, "Please, my lord...."

He peered intently at her through the darkness. Pulling her up to meet his lips, he gave her an enchanting kiss. He seemed surprised and delighted when he found her desire matched his own. His kiss intensified and reached into her very core, embracing her with passion. She kissed him hungrily, as though she was starving for attention and fulfillment. When he suddenly broke the kiss, she gasped at the denial she felt.

He placed his hand at the side of her face. "We must stop this before it goes too far." His breath was heavy, and when he meant to gently push her away and take his leave, she splayed her fingers beseechingly upon his chest.

"Please, my lord, do not leave me. I know what you would have from me this night, and I offer it willingly."

"You know not what you say, Gemma."

She leaned against him, the contact of their bodies soon making him forget any misgivings he had. She sighed when she knew he could no longer force himself to play the part of a chivalrous knight. He embraced her and again claimed her mouth in a desperate kiss. As he lay her back upon the bed, she whispered in his ear, "I am yours, my lord."

His kiss deepened, then his lips sought out the curve of her chin and neck. Kisses roamed her shoulders and sought her breasts as his hand stroked down her back and gripped her bottom.

Her back arched when his hot mouth latched onto her nipple. Her desire was so strong, so desperate, she ached to be fulfilled. As he trailed hot kisses from her breasts down to her belly, she entwined her fingers into his mane, silently urging him to put a swift end to her torment. Then he was again above her, and his mouth met with hers, their tongues joined in a fierce dance of desire.

He entered her slowly and gently kissed away her tears when he breached her maidenhead. The pain was fleeting and soon overcome completely by the urgent depth of her need. They lay joined together, locked in a passionate struggle as both sought to find release. Gemma soon felt her world explode. Tristan joined her in ecstasy, shouting his release to the heavens. Afterward, he lovingly kissed her sweet lips as they both curled up contently together and let exhaustion claim them.

~*~

As the dawn broke, the warmth of the rising sun mingled with the brisk wind reaching across the lands, drying the dampness of the eve's storm. The birds sang out their pleasure with the new day, and their songs awoke the two lovers, still locked tightly in an intimate embrace. They gazed deeply into each other's eyes, reveling in the glorious night they had spent showing one another their depths of desire.

Tristan reached out to brush a lock of hair from her face, which she had dropped to gaze shyly at the bed. He must have sensed her sudden unease now that the room had attained the morn's light.

"Gemma?" Her name sounded like a seductive caress the way he said it.

She lifted her head slowly to meet her lord's gaze. A satisfied smile tugged at the corner of his lips, and his eyes still held that feral look that told her quite clearly he had enjoyed their love-play, and would, mayhap, enjoy another taste.

"Good morn, my lord," she spoke shyly, a hesitant smile upon her lips.

"Good morn to you," he drawled. He made no move to get up from the bed, and when she grasped the blanket in her hands and made ready to escape, he lightly held her wrist so she could not. "A kiss before you make ready to leave surely would not be too much to ask?" His brow lifted with his seductive words.

Gemma leaned towards him and lightly brushed her lips across his. When he would have lingered and deepened the kiss, which surely would lead to further passion, she quickly wiggled away from him and practically leapt from the bed, with the blanket wrapped tightly around her.

"My lord, if you still insist I return with you to Haddon, I will offer you no more arguments. Indeed, I will admit my haste in fleeing and my rash request to remain here. It would seem I was not thinking clearly upon the matter, and I will submit to your wish that I return."

She suddenly felt foolish over her impulsiveness and began to think that returning to the castle was probably her wisest course of action. Too, she admitted to herself, after what they had shared last eve, she did not wish to be parted from him. No doubt, she was holding onto a fool's dream that somehow they may be together. She did not wish to be his whore, but she did not hold out false hope that there could be anything more to their relationship. Even now, as she looked into his desire filled blue eyes, she was suddenly afraid of the riot of emotions coursing through her. She loved him.

Aye, sometime last eve, after their joining and before she fell into a peaceful sleep, the realization had hit her. What could she now do but return with him to the uncertain future awaiting her at Haddon? For remaining here alone in her cottage was suddenly unthinkable.

Tristan rose from the bed and stood proudly and unashamed of his nakedness. He regarded her, appearing to be pleased over her sudden change of heart.

"Then let us make haste. We may make it back in time to join in the morning meal." He strode to the front room to don his clothing.

Gemma looked across the room and noticed the lid of her trunk lying open. She hurried over and peered within. To her dismay, she spied the journal resting upon the tousled blankets and gowns. Last eve when she had awoken, Tristan had been standing before the trunk, then he had joined her upon the bed. He had probably been searching for an extra blanket to wrap himself in and had uncovered the journal. Thank the gods she had awoken before he had a chance to discover its contents — that would have surely sealed her fate.

She quickly stuffed the journal beneath the blankets once more and decided she would not risk having it discovered at Haddon. Nay, she would leave it here at the cottage, where it may be safe.

~*~

Tristan turned around once again to urge Gemma onward. She was lingering over another batch of late wildflowers she had found in bloom. Once they had reached the roadway and left the forest behind, the ground appeared almost untouched by the eve's storm. The heat of the sun had set to warming the land by the time they'd been ready to leave the cottage, but Tristan had felt no real desire to hasten their journey back to the castle. Indeed, he'd enjoyed their time alone and the peaceful serenity he had experienced this morn at the cottage. After Gemma had agreed with him to return, he had suddenly felt loath to depart.

Haddon soon loomed before the pair as they rounded the last bend in the road. Gemma's hand, now resting lightly in the crook of his arm, tensed, and her grip became fierce. Noticing the hesitance in her, he placed his other hand comfortingly over hers. Looking down fondly upon her from his formidable height, he smiled reassuringly at her frowning face.

They approached the gate, and the portcullis was raised in anticipation of their arrival. They broke away from their companionable closeness as they passed beneath. Once again, he became the lord and she the peasant. As they made their way up to the castle doors, he felt a slight wave of unease settle over him. There were only a few workers and even fewer soldiers about this morn, and those who were tending to their tasks were casting fearful and anxious looks towards him.

The guard at the entrance of the castle nodded respectfully as he swung the doors wide to allow them entrance. Tristan strode ahead of Gemma towards the great hall, for he wished to break his fast and to speak with his men about the events of last eve. Of course, he would not relay all the facts, he thought, with a sudden quickening of his pulse.

He entered the hall, and a silenced hush came over the group. He looked around at the faces of his men and wondered what had happened, as the sudden silence was quickly met with a rush of excited voices seeming to be vying for his attention all at once.

"Silence!" he roared.

His brothers greeted him, and Denton began to announce excitedly the good fortune they had received last eve when two soldiers suddenly broke through the crowd. Tristan was stunned when he noticed they dragged a man between them. The man seemed strangely familiar to him, and as the prisoner lifted his head to face the Lord of Haddon, the realization of who he was struck him forcefully and unexpectedly. It was Madmont, the traitor, and before Tristan could utter a word, the man suddenly looked beyond him towards the door of the great hall. His face became deathly pale, and his glazed eyes began to bulge. He appeared terrified.

"You are dead!" Madmont screamed. "I saw your lifeless body, you devil's whore!" He then grew crazed and struggled with the guards, who held him tightly. "Talitha, be gone from me, do not look at me so! It was your own betrayal that led you to meet with your demise." The man collapsed to his knees, his head hanging low toward the floor as he silently wept.

Tristan turned around to see who had set Madmont off into such a state and came face to face with Gemma. She was staring at the man in horrified fascination. Her haunted gaze lifted to Tristan, and then she was gone, fleeing from the hall as if the hounds of hell were in hot pursuit of her.

CHAPTER 10

Tristan sat stiffly in his chair upon the dais. He looked grimly at the man before him, wondering why the traitor had returned to Haddon and what he had hoped to gain.

After chaos had erupted in the great hall, when Madmont had collapsed, and Gemma had fled, he had ordered everyone except his brothers and a few of his soldiers out of the room. He had sent the men holding Madmont to escort him to the dungeon so that he may learn how the viper had been brought into their midst.

His brothers described how they had ridden out last eve after Fury had been spotted at the gate without his master. They had thought to search for Tristan but instead had come upon a rough group of men lurking in the forest near Haddon. They'd been able to capture most of the miscreants, who were loudly boasting of their plans to overtake the castle. Deep into their cups, they had not offered up much of a challenge for the seasoned warriors, who quickly surrounded and overcame them. Some of the men had foolishly gone for their swords, only to be swiftly disarmed. But most of them had scattered, and since there were only eight in the group of Haddon soldiers, they could not capture them all.

Denton had boasted of how it was he who had run down the fleeing Madmont, and how he'd recognized him as the previous lord and traitor who had escaped Tristan a year ago. They had returned with their prize and had ushered him and his men into the dungeon. In the morning, they had brought Madmont to the great hall for questioning.

After hearing the tale, Tristan ordered Madmont be brought to him. Now the man stood defiant before the new Lord of Haddon, his hating stare portraying none of the earlier fear witnessed in him. Tristan regarded Madmont silently, watching for any sign that the man may again slip away into madness. But he did not appear to be senseless. There was a smug, calculating look upon his face as if he held some great treasure in his grasp. Perhaps he had earlier suffered from the excess of the eve's drinking? After spending a while below in the dungeon, he now appeared to have recovered from his earlier indisposition.

"Why are you here, Madmont? Is it the traitor's death you crave, or were you foolish enough to think you could retake Haddon from me?" Tristan's voice was deadly calm as the two men locked gazes.

Madmont was the first to drop his eyes. He spoke quietly, and Tristan had to lean over in his chair to hear the words that came forth.

"I have not come to reclaim that which was taken from me." He lifted his head to reveal a sadness upon his face. "Nay, my lord, I have come to beg the return of my most beloved daughter."

~*~

Gemma stood before the fire in her room, trying to gain control of her trembling body. The evil lord Madmont had returned to kill her, her thoughts screamed over and over in her mind. She began to pace around the room, her distress not allowing her to remain motionless. He had known her, she thought, absently running her fingers over the torc encircling her neck. Well, not her exactly, but her mother. But it would not take him long to piece together who she truly was. What would happen to her then? Madmont would surely claim her as his lost daughter, not wanting the humiliation of anyone knowing he suspected the child was not his own. Unable to prove who she was, would she be sent with Madmont to Edward to face a traitor's execution? It would be Madmont's final revenge upon Lady Talitha and Lord Tarquin.

She tensed at every sound she heard, thinking that any moment Tristan might send for her. He was probably right now interrogating Madmont and believing every evil word the man spewed forth.

A sudden knock upon her door made her jump, and she turned quickly, only to find Adele entering with a tray balanced upon her hip. The sympathetic look she gave Gemma revealed things were not going well below. Adele placed the tray upon the chair and opened her arms. Gemma did not hesitate to rush into them like a child. She wept in fear and frustration over the events that were happening. It was a bitter ending to the beautiful night she had spent learning the ways of love from a man who now, no doubt, thought her to be the evil spawn of the devil below.

"Adele," she cried. "What am I to do?"

"Hush, my child. All is not yet lost. Lord Tristan may not

believe what the man is telling him. He will come to ye, and ye must convince him Madmont is not your sire."

"Have you overheard anything from the hall, Adele?"

The servant looked guilty suddenly. "Aye, I took to listening at the kitchen door to what was being said. I could hear Lord Tristan demanding an answer from Madmont about what he was doing near Haddon. Oh, my lady! The evil, vile things that man told our lord. His soul will surely rot in hell for all the lies he has spoken."

Gemma gently pried herself free of Adele's sudden fierce grip. "Do you think I could escape? Surely with all the excitement below, no one would take note of me slipping out the gate."

"Nay, child. Since traitors have been captured so near the wall and with the chance of more about, the guards will be extra vigilant upon their watch."

Gemma paced fearfully before the servant. "What shall I do?"

"Ye must convince him that Madmont is a liar. Ye must tell him all, child, 'tis the only way."

"He will not be satisfied with only my word. I have no proof of that which I claim. He will think I have been in league with Madmont all this time. Nay, I fear he will judge me harshly. I fear he will send me to Edward as a traitor," Gemma said.

Adele quickly embraced her once more and made to leave the room. "I must not linger. Please, trust Lord Tristan. Tell him about Lady Talitha and Lord Tarquin, I beseech ye. He is fond of ye, I know. He must listen."

Adele left and shut the door behind her. Gemma sat down

on her bed and looked at the tray with no interest. How could she eat when the man she loved may send her to her death?

~*~

Tristan stood in his solar and stared out at the forest, scanning the trees for signs of Madmont's men. His brothers had pulled up chairs to the hearth to sit before the fire. The trio discussed the tale that Madmont had relayed earlier in the hall. His story had been so fantastic that Tristan had seen him returned to the dungeon so they may talk privately.

Madmont claimed he had lived in the forest with a few of his men since the night Tristan had overtaken Haddon. He did not want to venture too far away as he held out hope that one day his long-lost daughter would return to the castle. He claimed that many years ago, his wife's lover had killed her and taken his daughter. Madmont feared she had been abandoned in the forest but had held out hope she may still, to this day, be alive. He said over the years, since his wife's death, he had heard talk now and again from the villagers about a girl who lived with an old woman in the forest. Though acting as the village healers, there had been whispers they were in truth witches. The most important bit of information had been about a torc the girl wore, for his wife had worn a golden torc. But the night he had found her body, she did not have it on. He said he had looked everywhere throughout the castle, but surmised that the killer had taken it.

Just days ago, Madmont claimed, his men had overheard talk in Haddon's village that a young woman had been taken to live at the castle as a healer. He said he felt he had no choice but to try and gain entry to see if the girl was his daughter. He said he had never given up looking for her, nor the hope they would one day be together again. It was only the love of a father, desperate to be reunited with his daughter, that had made him risk the wrath of Lord Tristan, and even Edward himself. And now, after seeing her and mistaking her for his beloved Talitha, he knew his wait and his risks had not been in vain.

Madmont had begged Tristan to bring her to him so he may finally behold the daughter he had searched for these many years past. He had made quite an eloquent plea of saying he felt so ashamed of his earlier behavior towards the girl, and how he wished to make amends. He said it had been the shock of her resemblance to his dead wife that had caused him to become so overwhelmed with emotion.

Tristan had refused his request immediately; it not being his habit to grant boons to traitors. Instead, he had ordered him returned to the dungeon. The tight, smug smile upon Madmont's lips as he was taken away had unsettled him. He did not appear to Tristan to be a man who was a loving and concerned father. He needed to consider the information Madmont had relayed. Could it possibly be the truth? Could Gemma actually be that traitor's long-lost daughter?

Tristan walked over to join his brothers by the hearth, needing to voice the suspicions that flowed through his mind.

Giles regarded Tristan's somber façade. "Surely, you do not lend credence to what Madmont has said."

"I know not what to think. I am loath to admit there seems to be the ring of truth in his words. Yet, I cannot conceive how Gemma could possibly be the get of that monster."

"Be that as it may, the man knows too much about the girl for having just glimpsed her for so short a time, this you cannot deny," Denton said. "How knows he of the torc she wears?"

Tristan realized he had not been the only one to notice the adornment set around Gemma's pretty neck, though she had tried to conceal it. "This, I do not know," Tristan admitted in defeat.

"Too, I have heard talk around the castle, from some of the older inhabitants, of the resemblance of Gemma to Madmont's late wife. It would seem the evidence is enough to make Madmont's story ring true." Denton's opinion on the matter was apparent.

"If she is Madmont's daughter, it could be as he says, Tristan, that she knows naught of him and has indeed been lost to him these many years past," Giles said.

"Or it could be a way of protecting her. Perhaps they did know of each other. It could be she is a spy sent into our midst to help her father reclaim that which he lost. We may have foiled their plan, but he might be trying to make you believe Gemma is innocent of any plot so she may be free to help aid his escape," Denton reasoned.

"Nay, she could not be capable of such duplicity. Surely, Tristan, tell me you believe her innocent in this." Giles gave Denton a harsh glare.

Tristan ran his hand through his hair in an agitated gesture. He began to pace the hard floor as his thoughts ran wild. Could it be possible she had played him for a fool? What of her story of how she came to be at the castle? Was it the truth, or mayhap she had instigated the whole affair, the attack on her by Daniel and the story of her being in desperate need of aid? Last night might have also been part of her plan.

It was possible she had known all along that Madmont and his men were waiting for the right time to breach the walls of Haddon. It would make their task easier if Tristan was not there to lead his men. Tristan suddenly felt ill over what could have happened if his men had not found the traitors.

"There is only one way to discover the truth," Tristan said grimly. "I will question Gemma. May God help her if I find she had any part in this."

He strode out the solar door and headed down the hallway.

~*~

The door of her room crashed open, making Gemma jump up and prepare to flee as she looked into the steely eyes of Lord Tristan. He entered the room and shut the door behind him, leaning on the frame. She was trapped with the leopard, and he looked at her like a vile quarry to be devoured.

"My lord," she gasped fearfully. "Why do you regard me so?"

Tristan's face remained grim as he eyed her. "I have had the most interesting talk with the traitor, Madmont. He would have me believe you are his long-lost daughter."

Gemma had known this confrontation would happen. Still, she was unprepared for the fury of the man before her. She had witnessed the shock on Madmont's face when he had mistaken her for the wife he had killed. Given enough time to find reason for her presence, she knew Madmont would realize his error and would remember the daughter who had escaped his evil clutches so long ago. It was apparent he had told his story to Lord Tristan, no doubt trying to instill suspicion of her in his eyes.

"My lord, I know naught of this man except what I have seen for myself or heard in rumors from the villagers. I do know he is the old Lord of Haddon, and that he had been accused of treachery toward the king. But please, you must believe me when I tell you he is not my sire." Gemma tried to keep the tremor from her voice.

Tristan approached her and stood so close she had to lean back her head to look into his eyes.

"He said his wife was murdered by her lover and his daughter was taken from him. He says he has searched for years for her. Claims it is the reason why he remained hiding in the forests around Haddon, and why he came forth when he learned his daughter might be within these walls."

"I am not that girl, my lord," Gemma insisted. She could not believe the untruths Madmont had told about what had happened to her mother. It took all her restraint to not scream the man was an evil liar.

Tristan reached up to brush his fingers across the torc around her neck. "He knew of this. He said it was his wife's, and it had gone missing along with his daughter."

"I have told you, I know naught of my parents. My gran raised me and told me my parents were gone. Please, do not try to make me think the man that sits in your dungeon is my sire. I will never believe it."

Tristan grasped her tightly by the shoulders and pulled her up against him roughly. "I know not what to believe, Gemma. But until I sort out this mess, you are to remain under guard. You are not to leave this room unless I send for you. Do you understand?" he asked fiercely.

"Aye, my lord. I understand you have already made up

your mind, it would seem, and have condemned me," she said sadly. The formidable man before her did in no way resemble the gentle, loving man she had spent the night with.

~*~

After the evening meal, Tristan had not wished to remain in the company of his men, nor his brothers, and had instead decided to seek the privacy his room afforded him. After talking with Gemma, he had sent for a guard to be posted outside her door. The caution he'd been forced to take cast a sullen dampening over his mood. He felt fortunate over the capture of the traitor, but the victory was bittersweet, considering the tales the man had revealed.

Tristan sat before his desk with a quill poised in his hand, attempting to word a missive to the king. He was not certain he should mention Madmont's tale about Gemma. It would not exactly be withholding vital information, for, in truth, he could not verify what Madmont had relayed. However, if he did not mention the girl, and Edward listened to the man's rantings, it may not go well for Tristan to have withheld the information.

Tristan decided he would send word to Edward that he would dispatch the traitor to him in all haste. He would let the king decide what to do with the man, but Tristan was certain of the fate he was sure to meet. Traitors to the crown were dealt with severely and without mercy. What weighed heavily on Tristan's mind, though, was that the traitor's family, if not sentenced to meet with the same fate, could be stripped of title, lands, wealth, and sometimes imprisoned indefinitely.

Tristan could not bear the thought of Gemma being handed such a fate. She may be Madmont's daughter, but it did not necessarily mean she had been involved with him and his deception. He was determined to not let the passionate night they had spent in each other's arms cloud his judgment. He would tell Edward of the girl, but he would also relay his doubts on the matter. Too, he would not send Gemma to Edward when he sent Madmont. He would have to hope that Edward would allow him to deal with the girl himself.

Finishing off the missive, Tristan folded the parchment and affixed his seal on the wax. He rose from his desk and went to stand before the hearth. He was certain he had done the right thing in telling Edward of Gemma, but he could not quell the foreboding he felt. What if Edward demanded the girl be brought before him to face judgment? Tristan would have no choice in the matter but to comply with the king's order. There was no way he could protect her if Edward was decided on her fate.

Or was there? Edward would not imprison her if she became Tristan's wife.

Tristan began to pace the floor as his thoughts took flight. Aye, if they were to wed, she would be safe from Edward, for surely he would not pass harsh judgment upon her then. But to marry her? He had thought to one day take a wife and get himself an heir, but he was not yet even a score and ten.

Tristan went over other alternatives he could take, but none of them would offer Gemma the absolute protection she would receive if they were to wed. He had no other choice, not unless he wished to wait for Edward to decide what he would do.

Resolved, and now determined in the path that he would follow, Tristan stalked out of his room and headed down the passageway towards Gemma's guarded door.

~*~

The night was dark and chilled as winter crept ever closer to claim the land. The fall would be short this year, Gemma predicted as she stared out her window at the forest. Not that the seasons would matter very much to her if she were to remain a prisoner at Haddon. It may very well be that the dungeon would be her new home, and the change of the weather would not affect her in that dark prison.

She started as her door suddenly swung open, and to her surprise, Tristan stood towering in the doorway. The look upon his face was anything but pleasant, and Gemma concluded that he had come forth to relay his judgment upon her.

"Have you come to escort me to your dungeon, my lord?"

Tristan stepped inside the chamber and closed the door behind him. He turned to look at Gemma, his piercing gaze making her shake in sudden trepidation.

"I have made a decision." His voice was low, sounding like a growl. "I have written a missive to the king, informing him of Madmont's capture. I have also told him Madmont claims he is your sire."

"It is a lie, my lord."

"So you say, but you have not offered up any proof of your statement. Can you admit with all certainty he is not which he claims to be?"

Gemma hung her head in defeat. Telling him about the journal may condemn her more than help her. She could not be completely certain Lord Tarquin was her true sire, not with just her own feelings on the matter to guide her in her resolve.

This would not be proof enough for Tristan or the king.

"Nay. I know he is not my sire, but I cannot offer you the proof you seek. I can only offer you my word and what I know in my heart to be the truth."

Tristan crossed the room to stand before her. "'Tis not enough to save you from the wrath of Edward," he said softly.

Gemma backed away from him until she felt the opening of the window at her shoulder. She turned and closed the shutter, the brisk wind only adding to the chill she suddenly felt. "Then I am lost, am I not, my lord?"

Tristan turned away, seeming unable to face her. He walked to the door of the chamber but turned as he grasped the handle. "Fear not Gemma. I know of a way to save you from your ill fate. I have decided you shall become my wife." Then he was gone, shutting the door and leaving her to face his declaration alone.

"Wife?" Gemma whispered in shock. She must have imagined it—surely, Lord Tristan could not have just announced she would be his wife. It was impossible. But try as she might to make some other sense of his words, she had heard him right. How could she put a stop to this madness? He thought he would be keeping her safe from Edward's judgment, and she did not try to fool herself into believing he would marry her for another reason, like love. Nay, he was sacrificing himself for some misguided notion of chivalry.

Gemma felt her heart contract. She loved him, she knew it for certain, something she could not deny. But Tristan did not love her in return. How could he love her if he did not trust in her?

She could not allow him to go forth with his rash

decision—she must stop this somehow. Perhaps she could leave this place. She would find a way to escape the living nightmare her life had become. If only she could find Lord Tarquin and convince him she was, in truth, his daughter. If she could prove to Tristan that Madmont was not her sire, he would set her free. He could then find another woman, one he truly wished to wed.

Gemma paced the floor restlessly, plotting how she would make her escape. It had been easy enough the first time she had fled, but now she was no longer just the castle healer— now she was a prisoner. If she were able to get past the guard at her door, she would still have to get through the courtyard and beyond the wall. The gate was always well guarded— she would be challenged before she could exit. She needed a disguise. How would she manage it when she did not even have so much as a cloak to conceal her features? Maybe Adele could aid her. She also may be able to tell her where Lord Tarquin resided. The journal had relayed that his home was named Summit Crag, but she knew not what direction the keep was.

Gemma decided to make ready for bed, hoping sleep would clear her head of the riotous flow of thoughts and ideas racing through it. On the morrow, she would enlist the aid of Adele. Once she figured out how to escape the walls of Haddon and discover which direction to take, she would leave. She would not return until she had the proof she needed to set Tristan free of his noble sacrifice.

CHAPTER 11

High upon the ramparts, Tristan stood watching the departure of the traitor, Madmont, and his band of fellow outlaws. He had ordered his men to take the prisoners to London several days ago, but the sudden arrival of vicious rains and strong winds had delayed their leaving.

Tristan had endured the delay with trepidation, feeling the need to dispatch the enemy from his walls with all haste. The man's continued piety had worn on him, and he knew he would feel much relieved to be rid of his vile presence.

Tristan attributed the respite he suddenly felt to the sight of his soldiers finally fading from view, and with them the man who had thrown his life into such upheaval. He was still wary of what Edward's reaction would be when he learned that not only had Tristan failed to send along the traitor's daughter with her sire but that he had actually wed the girl. He had not yet done the deed, but by the time his missive reached Edward, he hoped to have done with the formalities. It worried him slightly to have not secured permission from his king with this decision. If he must, he would reveal to Edward his reasoning that he could not chance sending

Gemma away since she may, in fact, already be carrying the heir to Haddon.

Tristan was surprised, then apprehensive, when Cederic suddenly appeared at the doorway to the ramparts. He was breathing heavily as he approached, looking as though he had run up the steep flight of stairs.

"My lord!" He leaned heavily against the stone wall as he tried to regain his breath.

"What is it, Cederic?" Tristan had the feeling that whatever news Cederic brought him, it was not good.

"We found young Nicholas within the stables, bound and gagged. Someone has stolen his clothing, my lord."

"Bloody hell!" Tristan shouted as he began to race towards the stairs. Nicholas was a young squire to one of his knights who was part of the guard escorting Madmont to Edward and was to have joined his master on the journey. "Inform my men a prisoner has escaped, tell them to make ready to leave at once, and have Thad saddle Fury," he yelled over his shoulder to Cederic as he stormed down the stairs and headed through the passageway towards Gemma's room.

When he reached the door, he kicked it open and stalked within. His rage threatened to boil over when he spied Gemma's guard on the floor of the chamber. He bent over the man, relieved when he saw the rise and fall of his chest. At least she had not killed him. Tristan roughly shook the guard and was able to rouse him enough to pull him up to a sitting position. The man looked around the chamber, his glazed eyes finally coming to rest upon the terrible frown on his lord's face.

"What ails you, man?"

"I know not, my lord. Last thing I remember was late last night a maid came up and offered me a flagon of wine while I was tendin' the door."

"You were drugged," Tristan told him grimly.

He rose, and without another word, strode from the room. When he reached the stable, he found Thad and the groom rushing to prepare the horses to ride out.

Tristan approached Thad as he tended to saddling Fury. "Where is the lad, Nicholas?"

"In the yard, my lord, helping prepare the horses."

Tristan left Thad to his task and marched from the stable to seek out Nicholas. He spotted the boy leading a mount towards one of the soldiers. Calling out, he gestured to him to come forth. The boy handed the reins of the horse to the soldier and walked over to his lord. He hung his head as he approached Tristan, his manner clearly revealing his unease.

"Aye, my lord?" he asked, his voice quaking.

"What happened to you this morn?"

"I, ah...I was alone in the stable, preparing to ride out with the guards when I was hit from behind, my lord. Next thing I remember, I awoke to find myself buried in the straw, tied hand and foot, and gagged too, and stripped of all my clothing," Nicholas replied.

"Did you see your assailant?" Tristan asked coldly, already knowing the answer.

"Nay, my lord. I was hit from behind."

"That is all, lad. Be certain to have someone tend your head," Tristan told him as he strode towards Thad, who was leading Fury out of the stable.

"Did that already, my lord, when I went to get more

clothing," Nicholas called after Tristan's retreating form.

Tristan mounted Fury and turned to make certain the men who were accompanying him were ready to ride out. They were all mounted and eager to be off when Tristan gave the command to depart.

~*~

Gemma pulled the hood of the stolen cloak she wore tightly around her head. She rode last in the train of guards escorting Madmont on his final journey and had managed, so far by sheer luck, to have eluded discovery. Gemma was not overly proud of the way she had managed to escape the castle, nor the fact that the soldiers unknowingly had removed an extra prisoner from Haddon. The men were not riding hard, and for that, she was relieved, as she had never sat atop a horse unaided before and was finding she needed all her skill just to remain upright in the saddle.

She hung back in the line as far as she could, waiting for an opportune moment to break from the group who was journeying east to London. Adele had instructed her to head south until she reached the river, then follow it west until it led her to Calne. It was there she would find Lord Tarquin Alexander, if he still resided at Summit Crag Castle.

Gemma rode as slowly as she could without arousing suspicion, her thoughts wandering ahead to what might await her at her sire's castle. She hoped their meeting would be one of joy, not one of sadness and disappointment. She had been worried about what she would say to the man when she at last laid eyes upon him. Would he know her from sight, she wondered? Perhaps he might think she was a ghost, as Madmont had. If so, it would mean that he did remember Talitha, his lost betrothed, and it would surely prove to him that the lady was her mother. But it would not prove that he was her sire. It could take time to convince him, and unfortunately, time was something she was running dangerously low on.

~*~

Tristan and his men rode hard to catch up with the group of soldiers who had left Haddon barely an hour earlier. He rode with the grim determination of a man who, without a doubt, would recapture that which had fled him. This would be the last time he vowed that she would ever escape him. He appeased his ire with thoughts of how he would chain the vixen to his bed when he brought her back to Haddon. The thought of Gemma, helpless, awaiting his pleasure, set his mind to other more tantalizing thoughts of the nights they would spend together once they were man and wife.

So enraptured by his lustful thoughts, Tristan was startled when they came upon a group of riders on the road before them. They slowed their mounts as he and his men cautiously approached the unknown group. A rider urged his horse forward as he hailed Tristan with a friendly wave.

"Greetings, my lord. My men and I are in search of a band of outlaws who have been ravaging my lands over the past few months."

"Greetings. I am Tristan de Bohon, from Castle Haddon. Five days past, my soldiers captured a group of men found in the forest by my lands. By chance, they may be the same men you seek."

"'Tis possible," the man said, riding closer to Tristan. "I hail from Calne, just over a day's ride west of Haddon. I am

Tarquin Alexander, from Summit Crag Castle."

Lord Tarquin sat atop a huge white destrier. He was dressed all in black, which made his mane of white hair stand out. Despite his years, Tristan thought the older man to have the look of a seasoned warrior. Although he had just met Lord Tarquin and his group of soldiers, he took an instant liking to the man. It was good, he thought, to have a worthy knight for an ally. Tristan invited the group to accompany him and his men. He relayed how he just discovered that a spy might have infiltrated the guards, and he wished to inform his men.

Lord Tarquin agreed, saying it would give him more time to become better acquainted with Tristan, and allow him to see if the prisoners Tristan's guards were escorting were the same men he had been seeking.

~*~

Gemma had finally gained the courage to turn her horse off into the forest to escape the group when a sudden noise caught her attention. It sounded like a bird soaring past her ear. She thought it most likely just that when the man before her suddenly slumped over in his saddle. As he fell to the ground, Gemma's horse barely missed stepping on him. She veered her mount quickly to the side, and as she looked upon his crumpled form, she noticed the arrow protruding from his back. She screamed, but no one seemed to take notice of her as arrows suddenly began to let loose from the surrounding trees. The soldiers she accompanied rushed about, swinging their swords, ready for battle, trying to spot the enemy, but not able to stop the attack. The assailants held the advantage from being in the trees, and Gemma looked on in horror as she watched the ambush of the men around her.

Amidst the confusion, her horse seemed to acquire a mind of its own and ignored her feeble inexperienced attempts to control it. It took off towards the front of the group, past the men who were still uninjured and remained in their saddles. As her horse gained momentum and carried her almost to the edge of the forest and away from the attack, a strong arm suddenly swung out and snatched her from the saddle.

The ground flashed dangerously before her eyes when the unknown rider forced her face down over his mount. He rode away from the mayhem and skillfully guided his horse between the heavy column of trees on a winding path through the forest, leaving her breathless and lightheaded. It seemed like hours before the rider gradually slowed his horse to a walk, and then stopped altogether. Gemma felt the hand holding her in place grasp her roughly by the hair and pull her backward, tossing her like unwanted baggage to the ground below.

A sharp sting of pain in her ankle seized her as she tried to back away from the heavy, restless pawing of the horse beside her. Her head felt like it had struck the ground, so fierce was the pounding in her temples, most likely from being tipped over for such a long time. She shook her head and rubbed her hand across her eyes, vainly trying to regain her senses. Then she lifted her wary gaze to the person who had taken her on such a hellish ride. Her fear increased, and her terror took full rein when her eyes focused on the evil glare of the traitor, Madmont.

~*~

Tristan rode into the chaos his guards were facing, and quickly and efficiently took control of the situation. He ordered his men around the line of fire and into the forest to waylay the enemy, who were already fleeing, and to wait out the ones who remained in the trees that were quickly depleting their deadly supply of arrows.

Lord Tarquin's help proved invaluable, rallying his men to join with Tristan's in the search for the enemy and helping to aid the men who had fallen. Tarquin had dismounted to begin an assessment of the injured soldiers—who needed tending and who was lost to them. After Tarquin set some of his men to the task of dealing with the injured, he scanned the area to search out Tristan. Tristan saw him looking around and waved him over to where he knelt upon the ground next to a wounded guard.

"Who is he, my lord?" the guard asked Tristan at the unknown lord's approach.

Tristan got to his feet as he introduced the pair. "This is Lord Tarquin. We came upon him and his men on the road near Haddon. He hails from Summit Crag Castle of Calne. He is hunting the men who have been raiding his lands. He hoped the men he sought were the ones we had captured were the same."

"What happened here, man?" Tarquin questioned the guard.

"As I was saying to Lord Tristan, my lord, we were attacked. The enemy was hiding in the trees and waiting to ambush us. It seems it was a plot to free our captives. Unfortunately for us, it worked. Many of them rode off while we were dodging an assault," the guard answered.

Tristan's mood was ominous. He stood and surveyed the carnage before him with anger. When he had ridden upon the scene, sick terror had engulfed him. He had ordered his men to seek out the enemy, then he had dismounted and searched amongst the fallen men for Gemma. With every dead or wounded guard he encountered, a feeling of trepidation, then relief, encompassed him when he found it was not her. But where had she gone? Had she fled the group before the attack?

"My lord," the guard said, drawing Tristan's attention. "There is something else I must tell you."

The man's tone caught Tristan's attention, and he again leaned down to speak with him. "Aye, what is it?"

"Before the attack, just seconds before, I would have sworn I heard a woman's scream. I know it sounds strange, but too, as I lay upon the ground, I noticed a lad riding towards the edge of the forest, away from the battle. Probably a squire, as he seemed small enough, but I know not for certain for he was covered by his cloak. Then as the lad rode past, one of the traitors reached out and grabbed him right off his horse before riding away. I do not know why he would take the lad. Mayhap to secure safe passage? What think you, my lord?"

Tristan stood, and his eyes exchanged a look with Lord Tarquin's. This answered his question as to what had happened to the spy he was looking for. The girl had ridden off to freedom in the arms of her father.

Tristan strode over to Fury, ignoring the guard's question. Lord Tarquin caught up to him easily and placed a restraining hand upon his shoulder before Tristan could mount.

"I would join you if I may?"

"Aye, I would welcome your company, for I fear I might do great harm to the spy when I catch her," Tristan replied grimly.

Tarquin was startled by his statement. "Did you say *her*?"

"Aye, the little vixen that is to be my wife," he bit out before leaping upon Fury's back and riding off in the direction the guard had seen the traitor flee in.

~*~

Gemma rested against the trunk of a tree while she watched Madmont with anger. He had thrown her back upon his horse after revealing himself to her, then rode off again, fleeing further into the forest. Never had she been this far from the village—her surroundings were unknown to her, as was the direction they were taking. Mercifully, Madmont had allowed her to ride upright upon the saddle before him, his cruel arm encircling her waist in a tight embrace. They rode for a long while before he had finally reined in his horse, and again cruelly tossed her from the saddle onto the hard ground. The pain in her ankle was terrible, and she had quickly fallen to her knees, forced to crawl away from the horse to safety, the sound of Madmont's mocking laughter following her retreat.

As he secured his animal, she tore off a strip of the lining inside the cloak she wore to wrap her ankle. Madmont turned from the horse and began to saunter casually towards her. His smile was harsh and cold-blooded as he approached. "Well, my little daughter, have you a kiss for your sire?" he asked with amusement.

Gemma's smile, in return, was chilling as she watched him move even closer. The small dagger she held, retrieved from her boot and hidden within the long sleeve of the cloak, lent her much courage. The hatred she felt for him was beginning to outweigh her fear. Madmont leaned down and reached out his filthy hand to grab her arm and yank her up. She thought he would kill her, as he had killed her mother.

"Aye, *Father*, I have something to give you." She lifted the dagger.

Madmont's look of surprise turned to a growl of agony as Gemma plunged the dagger into his shoulder. It would have been his heart if he had not managed to turn slightly when she'd raised the weapon.

"You loathsome bitch!" he screamed, attempting to staunch the blood pouring from his wound. He grasped Gemma's wrist in a brutal grip, making her release the weapon. She attempted to flee, but with the burden of her injury, it took Madmont just moments to catch up to her. His bloodied hands grabbed her shoulders and shook her soundly. Raising his fist, he waved it threateningly before her face. "I should kill you for that," he snarled, shoving her roughly to the ground.

Gemma stared up at him with defiance. "As you tried to so many years ago? As you killed my mother?"

"Your mother was a whore," he sneered. "She deserved to die for her betrayal."

"My mother was *not* a whore! She was betrothed to Lord Tarquin Alexander. She was on her way to wed with him when you and your evil band of lechers set upon and killed them. You stole her from the man who is my true father. You knew I was not your child, that is why you finally murdered her and tried to do away with me."

"This time, I shall not fail." Madmont laughed insanely as he drew forth his own dagger.

~*~

The sound of arguing coming from ahead drew Tristan's attention. He slowed his horse to a walk, and Tarquin rode up alongside him.

"What is it, do you hear something?" he asked quietly.

"Aye, voices, over yonder." Tristan pointed towards the direction. The two warriors advanced cautiously, dismounted, and crouched behind a thicket as they watched the quarreling pair. Madmont loomed threateningly over Gemma with a dagger held in his fist. Blood now covered the other arm that hung uselessly at his side.

Tarquin's sights were aimed solely upon the man with the weapon. "*Madmont!* It is he who has been ravaging my lands," Tarquin hissed at Tristan. "I knew the old Lord of Haddon had been accused of treachery and escaped the king's justice. Over the years, I'd heard many vile rumors about him. Some said he had even murdered his own wife and child. I should have known it was the bastard who had been surviving by stealing from my people. I never actually saw the thief, but I had a good report on him, and I now see they are one in the same," he surmised. "What a fool I am for not making the connection sooner."

Tristan, seeing Gemma lying helpless before the monster, found it near impossible to remain hidden. What could have transpired here to make father and daughter suddenly turn on each other so? He watched Madmont carefully, ready to break free of the thicket in case the devil made a move to harm Gemma. But it would seem the man had much to say, for he stayed his hand and let his mouth run on.

"I knew you were alive. I have searched for you for years," Madmont sneered. He took a step closer to Gemma every time she managed to retreat from him. He appeared to enjoy seeing the fear upon her face.

"I escaped from your evil intentions before, and I shall do so again," Gemma vowed.

"What shall you do, girl, run away from me?" Madmont laughed. "Think you someone will come to your aid? Who would help you? A pitiful outcast, a witch from the forest?"

"I will," said Tristan as he advanced, his deadly gaze locked with Madmont's.

Madmont's face relayed his shock as Tristan drew forth his own dagger and approached him. "Would you slay me, my lord, a wounded man, for the sake of this girl? She has turned upon me, her own sire. It was her plan to slay your men and flee from you. She is a treacherous witch, my lord." The lie slipped easily from his lips.

"He lies," Gemma protested. "'Tis all lies he speaks. He knows he is not my sire, and he wishes to cast me into his betrayal."

"Look you at her, my lord. Even now, she plots and schemes to wile you with her whore's tongue." Madmont began to slowly back away.

"Silence!" bellowed Tristan. "I know not what has happened here, but I shall return you to Haddon, where I will hear the tale. Be assured you will answer to me for the deaths of my men you have caused this day." Tristan reached down to grasp Gemma by the arm, lifting her up to him. Their eyes met and held, and he felt his heart contract.

Something happened to him in that moment. An awareness of truth awakened inside of him, and he could no longer convince himself to deny what his heart had known all along. How could he believe such evil words from Madmont about Gemma? Her eyes glistened with unshed tears. He longed to take her into his arms and comfort her, for he knew in that moment he did believe in her. The coward creeping steadily away could not possibly have sired such a brave and beautiful creature. He led her over to lean against a tree and lifted her chin with his hand to gently press his lips upon hers. Then he gave her a quick wink before he turned away to deal with Madmont.

Madmont used the brief moment he was offered and took flight towards the thicket at the edge of the small clearing. His escape was cut short when Lord Tarquin suddenly appeared from behind the brush to confront him.

The two regarded each other, and Tarquin slowly withdrew his sword. "Shall we dance, you and I?" he asked, with a chilling smile.

CHAPTER 12

"Out of my way, damn you!" Madmont hissed, as he attempted to side-step around Tarquin's sword.

"I think not, knave, for we have much to settle between us." Tarquin moved in front of Madmont to block his path.

"There is naught between you and I," Madmont growled, becoming frustrated with the delay this man was costing him.

"Oh, I think there is. For are you not Lord Madmont, the ousted traitor of Haddon Castle?"

"What be it to you?" Madmont snapped as he continued his attempts to get past him.

"It is my lands and my people that you and your merry band of idiots have been harassing this past year."

Madmont stopped his movements suddenly, then looked intently at the man before him. Recognition finally registered, and he realized that this was not one of Lord Tristan's men. Nay, it was the bastard who hailed from Summit Crag. Another of King Edward's champions.

Madmont seethed with fury. It was *he* who should have been favored by his king, but it was Alexander who had endlessly won Edward's praise. Madmont glared upon the man before him, the man who held all of which should have rightfully been his.

"Let me tell you a story, *my lord*." Madmont smiled at Tarquin suddenly. He knew it was not a friendly smile, but one that looked to hold an evil secret. "There was once a knight many years ago, who journeyed from London in the cold winter months and took shelter along the way from a desperate, lonely widow at Haddon Castle. His one night's rest turned into a sennight, for the roads had become impassable from a sudden raging storm. During his stay, the knight and the widow became lovers. Though the widow had begun to care deeply for him, naught could come of their union, as the knight had already a young wife awaiting his return. The widow, though saddened to see him go, bid the knight farewell, for she knew he loved her not. And the knight took his leave, unknowingly leaving his seed planted deep within the widow's womb. The widow had been left with naught but a castle and loneliness for companions when her husband had died. So, upon discovering she was with child, she had been filled with joy. When she delivered a fine son many months later, she journeyed to seek out the knight at his home and show him the babe, which was his son. But the knight was not pleased. He was angry the widow had brought forth proof of his infidelity. He sent her away, his own wife having also delivered him a son."

Madmont paused, gauging the reaction from Tarquin. When he saw only confusion from his tale, he continued.

"The widow's bastard grew into a lad, and finally upon his mother's deathbed did he learn the name of the man who was his father. Over the years, he had begged his brokenhearted mother to reveal the man, but she would not. Not until she lay near death did she say his name...Aiden Alexander."

"What foul lies do you spew forth, Madmont? That is my sire's name, and I will not have you speak false of him," Tarquin raged.

Madmont saw the righteous anger that had come over Tarquin's face, only to be replaced by something else. Was it the acknowledgment of his father's perfidy?

"You are my half-brother, Lord Tarquin. I am the unwanted bastard our father would have kept secret. But alas, my lord, there is more to the tale. For have you ever wondered what became of the beautiful bride you were to have wed?"

Tarquin's head snapped up at the mention of his betrothed. "What would you know of my Talitha, Madmont?" he asked dangerously.

"Why, she became my bride, brother," Madmont said calmly, feeling almost giddy to finally be able to reveal to Tarquin how he had stolen away his intended and made her his own. He wanted to hurt Tarquin, just as he had been hurt over their father's denial of him. "It was I and my men who attacked her train when she crossed the border from Wales on her journey to become your wife. I did not love her, and I fear I treated her badly."

Tarquin's visage became one of rage. "How dare you, scum? You dared to steal my betrothed for the sake of vengeance against me? I knew naught of you. I knew naught of my father's betrayal, nor of another son he had. Why would you take revenge upon an innocent woman?"

"Fear not, dear brother, for the laugh was upon me. When I took her, she was not a maid, and too, she had your bastard resting in her womb." Madmont began to laugh insanely. "I killed her, I did, just as I killed your little bastard daughter."

Tarquin appeared numb with shock.

"When I heard from my spies that Talitha's mother and sire were seeking her out, I began to fear discovery. I sent forth some of my men to find her family and to kill them. They returned when the deed was done and told me they had set aflame their home. Talitha's sire was killed in the fire, but somehow her mother escaped. It was no matter, though, for I have yet to set eyes upon her."

"You killed them all?"

"Nay, like I said, the old woman escaped." Madmont smiled wickedly. "But you shall not, my lord." He lunged toward Tarquin suddenly, his dagger clutched tightly in his fist.

Tarquin's warrior instincts were too quick for him, and as Madmont lunged forward, he impaled himself upon the length of Tarquin's raised sword.

"May you rot in hell, dear *brother!*" Tarquin said as he watched the evil light dim from Madmont's eyes.

~*~

Tristan had watched Madmont flee. He did not give chase, as he knew Lord Tarquin would be there to see that justice was served. Instead, he turned his attention upon Gemma. She was regarding him with wonder as he bent down before her to examine the ankle she was favoring.

"Do you believe me then, my lord?"

"Aye, I do. It should have become clear to me sooner that the evil bastard was not your sire." Tristan stood up and took Gemma into his arms.

"I am glad you believe me, but I wish I could offer you proof, my lord."

"It does not matter. I am relieved you are safe and regret that if only I had believed in you, you would not have fled from me. Tell me, Gemma, does the thought of wedding me frighten you so?" he asked seriously, though a playful smile tugged at his lips.

"It was not wedding you that forced me to flee. It was the truth I sought. I wished to find the proof you required so you would not feel the need of making such a match with me."

"I wish to marry you because...I love you," Tristan said quietly, as he looked into her eyes.

Gemma hugged him tightly to her. "And I love you, my lord."

"Lord Tristan?" The pair unwillingly broke apart as they heard Tarquin's hail.

"Aye?" Tristan replied.

Tarquin came upon them, sheathing his weapon. "I hope you do not mind, but it seems your captive had a bit of a run-in with my sword. He's dead," he said with little emotion. Then his eyes took in the sight of Gemma beside Tristan, and he gasped. "Dear God, it cannot be."

Before Tristan could respond, Tarquin reached out a tentative hand and brushed his knuckles ever so lightly across Gemma's cheek. His eyes widened further when he noticed the torc encircling her throat. He said only one word. "Talitha?"

"What is it, man? You look like you have seen a ghost."

Tarquin ignored Tristan as he stared into Gemma's eyes. Eyes the same shade of green as his own. "Who are you, my lady?"

"I am Gemma, my lord."

"I am Lord Tarquin Alexander from Summit Crag Castle. 'Tis sorry I am, but you bear a startling resemblance to the woman I was to marry many years past. She was taken from me as she journeyed to Calne. I have just heard it from the viper's own mouth that it was he who had stolen her."

Gemma wiped a sudden tear from her eye as she regarded the man before her. "Lady Talitha was my mother. I am happy to finally make your acquaintance...Father."

"Father?" Tristan said, his look flashing between the pair.

"I am your father?" Tarquin asked in awe and confusion. "Madmont told me he had killed my daughter, along with my beloved Talitha."

"Aye, he did kill my mother, but I survived thanks to a faithful servant who secreted me away and brought me to the standing stones. My grandmother found me there, though I knew not who she was until I read my mother's journal. I have only just recently discovered that my mother had been stolen by Madmont, and of the foul deeds he committed against her and I. I had always thought myself to be an unwanted, abandoned babe until I learned the truth. But now I know, my mother did love me, and mayhap, Father, you too may come to love the daughter you were denied."

Tarquin embraced his daughter. "Had I known of you, my daughter, I would have come for you and brought you home."

"Will one of you tell me what is going on?" Tristan demanded.

"Please, might we return to Haddon? I promise I will

tell you both the tale. I am weary from my ordeal, and I wish to soak in a hot tub and enjoy a hearty meal," Gemma said, happily looking at the two men who regarded her in bewilderment.

~*~

The trio made their way over to where the knights' horses had been secured, Gemma between them both, her hands tucked securely in the crook of their arms.

"Oh, and by the way, Father, how would you feel about giving me away at my wedding?" Gemma asked Lord Tarquin as Tristan led her toward his horse. As he lifted her up into the saddle, Gemma felt such happiness. She had found her father this day, and she would wed with Tristan. Their union would not be one of necessity but of love.

EPILOGUE

FALL 1351

The young woman writhed upon the bed in the throes of agony. Her sweating brow was bathed with cool water from another, who bent over her.

"Push again!" Gemma urged the woman.

The woman complied, biting back a scream that begged to tear from her throat, concentrating all her effort on pushing the child from her aching body.

"That's it! Push. Push," Gemma again demanded, until finally, into her hands, was delivered a tiny child.

The woman collapsed upon the bed, breathing heavily, momentarily delirious with relief from being free from pain. She had labored hard for several hours, her pains coming on in the early afternoon of the previous day. Quickly she had taken to her bed, nearly doubled over with the force of her contractions. Now all she wished was to see her child. She had wanted this child more than anything in the world. Wishing and praying for it forever, it would seem.

"Please, let me see the child, Gemma," she begged.

Gemma hurried to complete her ministrations and place the swaddled infant into the waiting arms of his mother. "You have a son, Judith," she said, smiling through tears in her eyes.

Judith crooned to the boy, delighted with the thatch of dark curls upon his head. She lightly brushed her fingers over his pink cheek, her vision blurring with tears of joy of her own. She raised her eyes to Gemma, who was busy tidying the small cottage and opening the shutters over the windows to allow the fresh morning air and light within. It was guilt and regret Judith now felt. She had refused to allow Daniel to summon Gemma, and he had complied, until the pains had become so great, he had not known what else to do. He had told her that none could aid them in the village, and in any case, he would trust no other to deliver this child.... His child.

In the autumn of the previous year, Judith's husband had become ill. Judith had attended him herself, not daring to seek help from the new mistress of Haddon. How she had hated Gemma for marrying Lord Tristan. And how it had angered her even more greatly when most of the villagers had begun to lose their fear of the former "witch of the forest." They had gone forth to Haddon in search of her when sickness or pain had plagued them. Gemma had administered to them with no mention of their earlier strife or distrust.

Judith's husband had succumbed to his ailment not long after, and she had been filled with despair over the loss. She had gone on with her life and was surprised when Daniel had approached her just two months later to ask for her hand. She had accepted, for being alone in the world, she was somewhat lost. There had always been her husband to rely upon, and she did not enjoy her life of loneliness. Soon, much to her surprise, she had found herself with child. It had been a fearful first few months of pregnancy, for, in the past, she had miscarried every time. But this time, it was not to be so. The child thrived within her womb, and Judith had grown large and heavy as the months crept by.

She had been overcome with pain when Gemma finally entered her cottage to give aid. Daniel had gone to his wife's side and begged her forgiveness for summoning the mistress of Haddon. He had comforted her by saying his love for her was so great he could not bear to lose her, nor their child. Judith had been angered over Gemma's presence in their home, but there had been naught she could do except writhe upon the bed with her agony. She had labored long and was exhausted. At this stage, she would have accepted help from Lucifer himself if he had offered her his aid.

"Gemma, please," Judith said, gesturing for her to come closer.

Gemma approached her and offered a cup of cool ale to satisfy her thirst. Judith accepted the cup while holding her tiny son nestled in the crook of her arm. "M'lady, I fear I have wronged ye greatly. I beg ye to forgive me."

Gemma smiled at Judith. "I, too, have been quick with sharp words, Judith. I accept your apology, and I would be very happy if we were to be friends, at long last."

Judith returned the smile. "Aye, m'lady, friends we shall be."

~*~

Gemma turned to walk towards the doorway, wiping a stray tear from the corner of her eye. The miracle of birth

had never ceased to amaze and overwhelm her. She turned
to look upon the scene of mother and child before she left the
cottage, a smile of contentment on her face.

As she stepped outside, Daniel approached her. His eyes
were red rimmed with vestiges of a restless night upon them.
"Gemma...m'lady. How fares my wife and child?"

"They are both well, Daniel. Resting within, and anxious
to see you, I might add." Daniel smiled his thanks and quickly
rushed within the cabin to finally lay eyes upon the child he
had long waited for.

Gemma climbed upon her waiting mount and started out
at a slow pace towards the castle. As she ambled through the
village, the rousing peasants shouted their cheerful morning
greetings as she passed them by. Gemma returned their
waves and pleasant greetings, feeling at long last a sense of
belonging. It was strange, she reflected, thinking of how she
had yearned to always be one of the villagers. Though now,
by becoming their lady, she still was not a part of them, but
she had found acceptance among them. And it was enough.
So great was the joy in her heart, which was filled with love,
there was no room for bitterness.

Instead of heading directly to Haddon Castle, Gemma
decided to turn her mount off the roadway and enter the
forest. She journeyed on for a way through the trees until she
came upon a clearing. Here she tied her horse and continued
on foot, climbing the small slope that was home to the
standing stones. She circled their colossal formations, then
made her way to the center of them. She began to dance. Her
hips swayed to a rhythm only her gifted ears could detect as
she softly sang the ancient words of her ancestors.

It was here that Tristan found her, just as he had found her a year ago, changing both of their lives forever. He tied Fury beside her mount at the edge of the forest and walked over to stand at the base of the slope. Gemma felt the heat of his stare upon her. She gazed at Tristan, her husband, her love. She did not end her dance — she continued to move her body in rhythm to her song. Soon, she would not be able to move with such grace and agility. Before long, her own body would begin to grow heavy with the child beneath her heart that she and Tristan had created with their love.

But for now, as Tristan looked upon her and she danced within the circle of the standing stones, she would bask in the love that shone in his eyes and know that her gran's long-ago vision of her destiny had at last been fulfilled.

ABOUT THE AUTHOR

Julie is a long-time resident of Hamilton, Ontario, where she lives with her husband of 25 years. She has two grown sons who recently left the nest. Working in a library for several years inspired her to pursue her long-time love of writing. Please check out her website http://julieparker.yolasite.com/

www.ingramcontent.com/pod-product-compliance
Lightning Source LLC
Chambersburg PA
CBHW030331180626
46810CB00003B/1306